An Orphan for Nebraska

Charlene Joy Talbot

An Orphan
for Nebraska

Atheneum · New York

"Little Old Sod Shanty on the Claim," on page 110,
is from *The American Songbag* by Carl Sandburg,
published by Harcourt Brace Jovanovich, Inc.

LIBRARY OF CONGRESS CATALOGING IN PUBLICATION DATA

Talbot, Charlene Joy.
An orphan for Nebraska.

SUMMARY: Orphaned on the journey to America in 1872,
a young Irish boy finally makes his way to Nebraska
where he goes to work for a newspaper editor
and learns to do the work of a printer's devil.
[1. Orphans—Fiction. 2. Frontier and pioneer
life—Fiction. 3. Nebraska—Fiction] I. Title.
PZ7.T1418Or   [Fic]   78-12179
ISBN 0-689-30698-9

Atheneum
Macmillan Publishing Company
866 Third Avenue, New York, NY 10022
Collier Macmillan Canada, Inc.

Manufactured by Fairfield Graphics, Fairfield, Pennsylvania
Designed by Mary M. Ahern

7 9 11   13 15 17 19   20 18 16 14 12 10 8

For Celine and Maya,
and with thanks to Doris Portwood
for the idea of orphans
in Nebraska

Contents

An Orphan for Nebraska

1

America!

"**L**and ho!"

Kevin O'Rourke heard the shout in his wooden bunk in the bowels of the ship. He raised himself cautiously, remembering the wet beam only inches from his face. The beam supported the deck above, and he had already bumped his head on it too often.

"America!" a sailor shouted down the hatch. Faint morning light filtered through the opening.

"Praise be to God!" cried Mrs. Murphy from the bunk below Kevin.

"—and all his holy saints!" said another voice. Cries and groans of thankfulness rang from every corner of the fetid darkness.

Kevin delved under his blanket for his britches. While he pulled them on, he heard a wild scramble at the ladder leading upward as men and children hurried topside.

Kevin slid down the rough bunk ladder until his feet touched the cold, damp wood of the steerage deck. Tying his britches as he ran, he joined the stream of fellow immigrants tumbling up into the gray dawn. He gained the deck and found a place at the rail. Behind the ship the October sun was squeezing through the mists of the horizon. Ahead Kevin could see nothing but the gray Atlantic Ocean.

"Where?" cried the first of the women, coming up to join the menfolk and children.

"The devil take you—" In her disappointment Mrs. Finn shouted at a sailor. "There's no land!"

"I see no land!" others began to exclaim. But some of the men had been fisherfolk and knew what to look for.

"It's not mountains you're looking at, nor the green coast of Killarney, but yon gray line, that thread, see, at the bottom of the sky."

"I see it!" a child shrieked. The child's father laughed and swung it to his shoulder.

A lump caught in Kevin's throat. Others were

beginning to see the land, or say they saw it. Kevin *thought* he did. It looked impossibly far away, but the engines were throbbing and a brisk breeze was filling the sails. Around him everyone began to laugh and shout and hug each other. Mrs. Murphy kissed all of her children within reach. Seeing Kevin, she kissed him, too.

"Ah, your blessed mother," she cried. "She'll be looking down from Heaven with tears of happiness."

Kevin nodded, but suddenly he felt frightened. He made his way aft and sat on a coil of rope. People were hanging over the rail, willing the thin line to grow closer.

Mary Finn, whose mother had shouted at the sailor, came to sit beside Kevin.

" 'Tis a shame your mother did not live to see it," she said. "Such a lady, she was."

"She's happier with my father," Kevin said gruffly.

"And what about you?" Mary worried.

"I've my uncle," he told her. "The one who sent the tickets."

"That's well, then."

"Besides, I'm old enough to take care of myself, if there's work, as they say."

"Are you now?" Mary gazed at him solemnly. Kevin stared back at her, trying to see her as people in America would. Matted hair, the same red as his own, thin face the color of dough, except for the sprinkling of freckles and the dark circles beneath her blue eyes. Her dark heavy skirt was ragged and torn at the hem, but so were Kevin's britches. Her bare feet, like his, were chapped and grimy. He would put on his shoes before he landed, and his jacket.

"I'm eleven," Kevin told her.

Mary was considering him as though she, too, were looking through the eyes of a stranger and was not impressed with what she saw.

"Eleven are you? You're small for your age."

"And I can read," Kevin reminded her. Among the unlettered Irish peasants, he was considered something of a prodigy. Only priests could read, and schoolteachers from the city. Kevin's father, Timothy O'Rourke, had been a schoolteacher until the lung disease killed him, leaving his wife and son to fend for themselves. They had done a poor job until Kevin's mother's brother, wild Michael O'Halloran, had sent them steamship tickets from America.

Kevin had made himself popular aboard ship by

reading aloud the advertising flyers the American railroads were distributing all over Ireland.

MISSOURI IS FREE!
Farm Homes in Northern Missouri.
Hannibal & St. Joseph Railroad offers for sale nearly 500,000 acres of the finest prairie, timber and coal lands in the West! Land is sold in 40-acre lots or more on two or ten years' credit at prices ranging from $2.40 to $10 an acre.

Most of the immigrants, like Kevin, were lucky if they had two coins to rub together, but it was marvelous just to hear about the opportunity, coming as they did from a country where land was never for sale, unless great landlords traded among themselves. Even the churchyard had to be used again and again, the bodies buried atop one another. A man couldn't even have a grave to himself.

"They say schools here are free for everyone," Mary murmured. "Is it hard to learn, Kevin?"

"Didn't I teach you most of the letters?" Kevin said. "But one needs a slate, and a pencil to write on it."

Mary's mother called to her to come and mind the baby while she took her place in the washing-up line.

Kevin sat on the coil of rope and thought about what would happen next. He realized with dismay that he'd been very safe on the ship. Even though his mother had been buried at sea, he had been surrounded by his countrymen, snug as a herring in a barrel. Now, when the boat docked, the barrel would be opened, and the passengers scattered, some perhaps actually going to the West. Except for Uncle Michael, Kevin would be alone among Americans.

"Michael O'Halloran would be a thin reed to lean on," Father had said when he was alive and Michael's letters had urged them to come to America. But after Father's death, when Mother and Kevin were near to starving, hadn't Uncle Michael sent the tickets?

Kevin was glad when the breakfast bell rang. Everything was welcome that made the time go faster. It was hard to sit still and keep out of the way, but running about the deck made the sailors swear. They weren't above cuffing you out of their way, either.

When Kevin and Mary finished their bread and

coffee and trooped up on deck again, land could be seen clearly.

People returned to the steerage, rejoicing that it was for the last time. They began packing and bringing their meager bundles up to the deck, eager to leave the reeking hole where they had been shut in for days while bad weather raged. Kevin went down, too. In his bunk he rummaged through his mother's bundle till he found the comb. He forced it through his tangled red hair. Everything he owned had to be kept in the bunk; not that he owned much, his mother's bundle and his combined made little more than a handful. Before the tickets came, they had already sold almost everything they owned to buy food.

Kevin's shoes were damp and stiff, but he eased his feet into them and went back on deck.

Even the people who had been sick were getting dressed. No one must arrive sick in America. The men related stories of what happened if you did arrive sick, but they were hardly listened to because, miraculously, everyone who had survived the voyage was well, or pretending to be.

The boat made its way upriver. By the time it docked the travellers were worn out from staring.

Sailors pointed out the green shores of Staten Island and New Jersey, the house-dotted shore that was Brooklyn.

The immigrants were not allowed to land on the pier. Instead they were herded onto a barge. With their baggage, they were taken back downriver.

Castle Garden, at the end of Manhattan island, was the gateway. Here, at last, they set foot on American soil. Some of the women, among them Mrs. Murphy, knelt on the dockside to give thanks.

In a hubbub of excitement and laughter, carrying bags and bundles, they straggled into the vast circular building.

Kevin had never seen so many people in one place, and all milling about, talking and shouting. Would Uncle Michael be among them? Through the cries of joyous recognition from waiting relatives, Kevin heard the babble of foreign tongues. His mother had not been sure whether Uncle Michael could meet them, but Kevin had the address of his rooming house. Having come so far, he was sure he could make his way there, though New York City was ten times the size of Cork, where he had boarded the ship.

A great fountain in the center of Castle Garden

was surrounded by desks, and the travellers from Ireland were waved into lines before these. Uniformed men moved up and down the lines, looking into some of the baggage while the line inched ahead. The first line brought them to doctors who made sure no one arrived with any dreadful diseases, like smallpox. The second line brought them to a row of clerks. Kevin's turn came at last.

"By yourself?" asked the man behind the desk.

Kevin nodded. From the Murphy family in back of him, Mrs. Murphy spoke up.

"The boy's mother died of ship fever, God rest her soul."

"Let the boy answer the questions, please," the clerk said. Mrs. Murphy stepped back with a grumble. Officials were alike the world over.

"Name?" snapped the clerk.

"Kevin Thomas O'Rourke."

"Birthplace?"

"Limerick, in county Limerick."

"And where in the world might that be?" The clerk looked up with a twinkle.

"Ireland," Kevin said proudly.

The clerk took his age, his mother's name and his father's.

"Read and write English?"

"Yes."

"And who's to keep you off the streets here?"

"My uncle, Michael O'Halloran."

"Is he here?"

"I don't know yet." Kevin looked vaguely at the streams of people.

"Do you have his address? Let me see it. Ah, Baxter Street. I might have guessed. Well, you won't have any trouble finding that. See that you stay out of trouble when you get there!" He spoke aside to a man in a different kind of uniform: "What can Ireland be like, if Baxter Street and the Five Points are an improvement?" He turned back to Kevin.

"How much money do you have?"

When Kevin's mother lay dying aboard ship, she had used the last of her strength to stitch their few precious coins into the waistband of Kevin's britches.

"Nine shillings sixpence," Kevin said as his fingers felt them.

"You can't use English coins here, you know," the clerk told him. "You'll have to exchange them for American money. See that booth?" He pointed. "That's an official money changer. No doubt your mother stitched the money in your britches?"

Kevin felt his face burn. How had this stranger guessed?

"Go over there to the men's room and take it out. When you get it exchanged, ask a policeman to tell you how to get to Baxter Street. Have much to carry?"

Kevin held up his blanket-wrapped bundle.

"That's not much. You can walk to Baxter. Don't get involved with any sharps. Next!"

Kevin felt himself dismissed. Did that mean he was now in America? Apparently as soon as he exchanged his money he was free to go.

Following the clerk's instructions, he got out his shillings, handed them over, and received some paper money, and some silver and copper coins. He no sooner pocketed them than a green-hatted man was at his elbow.

"Ah, me boy! How are you?" The man held out his hand.

Kevin shook it and looked wonderingly into his face. He hadn't seen Uncle Michael for more than two years, but he thought he remembered him. This couldn't be he! Uncle Michael was young and slim. This man looked Irish, though—blue eyes, black hair, the green hat.

"It does my heart good to see you, fresh from the Old Sod," the man was saying. "I was fresh off the boat meself not long ago, and I'll tell you I'd have been happy to speak to some soul as knew his way about. I says to meself, as soon as I learn, I'll spend all my free time helpin' newcomers. How can I help you, sonny?"

"Did Uncle Michael send you?" Kevin asked, puzzled.

"To be sure he did!" The man took hold of Kevin's arm and urged him toward the board fence that surrounded Castle Garden. "Now where does Uncle Michael want us to go?"

Before Kevin could show him the Baxter Street address, a uniformed officer with a nightstick loomed above them.

"Sam!" He poked the nightstick into the man's ribs. "Is not even a child safe from your scurvy tricks? Off with you!"

The green-hatted man muttered, pulled the hat over his eyes, and scuttled away.

Watching him disappear, Kevin felt a pang of disappointment. "He said he was from my uncle!" he exclaimed.

"I'll bet he did, the wicked liar! And did he,

perhaps, see you put a bit of money into your pocket?"

Kevin was too shocked to reply.

"You'd best find your uncle yourself." The policeman pointed out Broadway, told Kevin to walk to the park at City Hall and inquire again, but only of a policeman. This was no city in which to trust strangers, he warned.

Kevin thanked him and looked around for the Murphys or Mary Finn—someone to say goodbye to —but they were nowhere to be seen. He suddenly felt terribly young and alone. How disappointing that Uncle Michael had not sent someone! But if he lived so close, no doubt it wasn't worth anyone's while.

Kevin shouldered his bundle and set off up Broadway. The sidewalks were crowded with people. Streams of horsedrawn vehicles filled the streets. Kevin cast a hopeful glance at the cobblestones. They were the same as Limerick cobblestones, and no pennies were lying in the cracks. He had not exactly expected to find pennies on the streets, but people did say. . . . A pair of ragged boys selling newspapers caught his eye. If there had been money in the streets for the picking, those boys would have gathered it.

The buildings were no taller than the ones back in Cork. The high-rising church spires made good landmarks. Near the second spire a policeman pointed the way to the park. Kevin crossed it and found himself in a warren of dirty, smelly streets, one of which was Baxter.

He found the rooming house whose address he had, climbed the steps to the door and knocked. It was opened by a tired-looking woman with a crying baby on her arm.

"I've come to see Michael O'Halloran," Kevin announced.

"And who might you be?"

"His sister's son, from Limerick."

"Just off the boat?" She didn't sound surprised. The baby cried harder. She held the door wide. "Come in."

Kevin stepped into the hall and let his bundle fall.

"Michael O'Halloran said your mother was coming with you."

Kevin nodded. "She—" He choked. Uncle Michael, too, would have to be told. He raised his voice above the baby's yells. "She took the ship's fever. She didn't live through it."

"Ah, the poor thing!" The woman crossed herself. "Hush!" She shook the crying baby. "And you, poor boy, I have bad news, too. Mick O'Halloran's in jail."

2

Uncle Michael

Jail! Kevin's heart thudded. A sob rose in his throat, but to cry before the woman was unthinkable.

"Why?" Kevin managed to get the word out.

"Ah, 'twas bad. 'Twas working on the bridge he was—the new bridge to Brooklyn. Mick flung his spade at the foreman, and the pesky man took a heart attack and died. 'He called me "paddy" once too often,' Mick told the judge, but the judge gave him two years."

Two years! Father was right: Uncle Michael was a weak reed.

"You can visit him on Sunday. That's tomorrow,

ain't it?" The woman sounded a bit more friendly. The baby subsided into hiccoughs.

A chill was sinking into Kevin's mind. He was completely alone! In a city where he knew no one.

"Mick's room is empty, if you've a mind to rent it." The woman looked hopeful.

Kevin hesitated. A room that had been Uncle Michael's, connected to someone familiar . . . He fingered the folded bills and the coins in his pocket.

"How much would the room be for a week?" He had to sleep somewhere.

She named a sum. He had more than that in his pocket, but he would need to buy meals, too, and he had no idea what things cost in New York.

"All right," Kevin told her.

As he followed the woman upstairs, he thought how ashamed his mother would have been to find her brother in jail. At least she had been spared that. Even back in Limerick folks had called Michael O'Halloran wild. But I'll visit him in the morning, he said to himself. He'll tell me how to get on.

The house held the familiar smell of cabbage. Kevin began to feel better.

The woman led him up two flights of worn stairs to one of the rooms in the attic. In the room was a stool and a broken wooden bedstead with a thin mattress.

" 'Tis safe to leave your things here," she said, eyeing Kevin's bundle. She fished about in her apron pocket and produced a key. The baby made a grab for it, but she put it in Kevin's hand. "My name's Mrs. Riley." She told him he would find a pump and the necessary in the back yard.

Alone in the room Kevin sat on the bed and listened to her retreating footsteps. The house felt empty; the other lodgers would be at work. He had gotten over the shock about Uncle Michael. He no longer wanted to cry. In fact, he felt excited. He was actually in America, where there was said to be work for all. He thought of the boys he had seen on the street selling newspapers and shining shoes, and one delivering a package.

He spread his blanket over the mattress and stood looking at his mother's bundle. Almost everything they owned had been sold to pay for the journey from Limerick to Cork, where the sea voyage began. The bundle contained a comb, a hand mirror (a gift from Kevin's father), her other dress, Kevin's spare shirt, her marriage certificate, her prayerbook and a bar of soap. He wished he'd given the prayerbook to

Mary Finn to remember him by.

Suddenly he realized he was hungry. It was late afternoon; he had eaten nothing since breakfast. He turned the key in the lock, put it in his pocket, and ran downstairs.

From the doorstep he looked at the noisy scene. Rows of pushcarts lined the gutters and crowded onto the sidewalk. Between them horse-drawn wagons with iron-tired wheels clattered and rumbled. And people were everywhere—shouting, selling, buying, hanging about. There seemed to be as many people in this one street as in the whole town of Limerick.

Kevin selected a meat pastry and an apple from a pushcart and took them back to Mrs. Riley's doorstep. He sat there to eat and watch the goings-on.

When he finished, he found his way down a garbage-filled passage beside Mrs. Riley's house to the back yard and the pump. He pumped himself a drink and washed his hands. Back here, behind the houses that fronted the street a second row of dilapidated dwellings were crowded onto the backs of the lots. High board fences closed them off from their neighbors. In the yard where he stood was a row of privies, the pump, two pigs in a pen and a million buzzing flies.

Kevin had not dreamed a city could be this crowded, but he dared not let himself remember the countryside about Limerick. If one could eat greenery, Ireland would be the perfect place to live. Beauty, unfortunately, was not edible.

He decided to acquaint himself with the neighborhood. The ground floor of every house held at least two small, dark shops. Most of them sold second-hand clothing and household things. A few sold groceries.

At the cross street three of the corners sported grog shops. As Kevin approached, a small, barefoot girl flitted out of the nearest one, carrying a pitcher brimming with ale. Before Kevin could move, she plummeted into him, slopping ale onto her shawl and her bare feet.

"Cantcher look where you're going!" she snarled. "Stupid paddy!" she added, noting his red hair.

Kevin shrank against the building, looking right and left to see if anybody was watching. The girl scuttled on down the sidewalk and disappeared between two buildings. Nasty-tongued little thing! People seemed ill-mannered in this city.

He continued on his way with more caution.

The surrounding streets were as busy and clamorous as Baxter Street. He saw two people—an old man and a child of five or six—rooting in the piles of garbage, searching, apparently for food. The sight promised ill. Was there really work here?

He made his way around four sides of the block, back to where he started. He hated to end his first day in America by tamely going to sleep, but he was too tired to walk further. His eyes ached from staring.

Wearily he climbed the stairs. In his room he bolted the door, removed his shoes, wrapped himself in his blanket and lay down on the lumpy bed. The noise outside had not lessened with darkness. Horses, wagons and pushcarts still rumbled over the cobblestones. People were still shouting and quarreling.

THE NEXT THING he knew light was filtering through the small window. He slid out of bed and ran shivering down to the back yard. Mrs. Riley was there. While she waited her turn to pump a bucket of water, she told him how to get to the penitentiary on Blackwell's Island. Kevin would have preferred to be given the directions in a less public place, but the man and two women also waiting their turns at the pump did not appear shocked. In fact, they seemed to know the cheapest way as well as Mrs. Riley. She told him to take the horsecar to Ninety-second Street and walk east to the river, where a boat could be found almost anytime.

"Be sure you take him some tobaccy," she told Kevin. "Aye, and some apples, too. Buy them here, mind. Everything's more expensive uptown." Her neighbors nodded sagely.

Back in his room Keven put on jacket and shoes. He considered taking his mother's prayerbook to Uncle Michael; it would do Uncle Michael good. The trouble was, he couldn't read.

Kevin bought tobacco and apples and paid his fare on the horsecar. The trip uptown took almost two hours, and in all that way the streets and houses never came to an end. At last the horsecar reached Ninety-second Street. Kevin and several other people got off and walked to the river.

At the pier an old woman in a shawl was selling hot rolls and coffee. By now Kevin was so hungry he was happy to pay the few pennies she asked. Nevertheless, he realized how fast his store of coins was melting away. The sooner Uncle Michael told him what to do, the better.

The boat was waiting, and a man helped Kevin

climb aboard. The rowers were dressed alike in jackets and pants with wide black-and-tan stripes. Caps covered their heads. A woman said they were prisoners. Kevin studied them covertly. Uncle Michael might be among them, but he was not.

The boat trip would have been pleasant had it not been for the penitentiary looming ahead. Gloomy wings stretched out to either side of the square central tower, the whole decorated with round turrets and notched battlements like an ancient Irish fortress. The passengers avoided each other's eyes, as though they themselves had done something shameful. When the boatmen set them ashore on the island, the other people, mostly women, seemed to know where to go, and Kevin followed. The tobacco and apples had to be inspected before the guard could take him to Uncle Michael. He was led down a long corridor, past dozens of cells. Visitors stood outside some of them. Kevin's heart was beating as hard as though he himself were being locked away.

At last the guard stopped. "O'Halloran!" He clanged his ring of keys on the bars of the cell door. "Visitor."

A man with a shaved head appeared on the other side of the bars. Kevin did not recognize him.

"Kevin, lad! 'Tis glad I am to see you!"

Uncle Michael! And in such disgrace! Kevin burst into tears.

"Stop that, boy!" Uncle Michael ordered. " 'Tis not the end of the world."

Even while he sniffed and tried to stop crying, Kevin wondered how Uncle Michael could say that. Two years! It *was* the end of the world.

"Where's your mother?" Uncle Michael was demanding. And Kevin had to tell him.

After that, the shoe was on the other foot: Kevin had to try to cheer Uncle Michael. He brought up the problem of what he was to do with himself. While not cheerful, it did give a turn to the conversation.

"How much money have you, dear boy?" Uncle Michael asked. "A little cash would greatly improve things here. Can you spare some?"

"Of course!" Hadn't Uncle Michael saved all his money to send the steamship tickets? Kevin would willingly have given him all he had. He brought it out, but Uncle Michael told him to keep half. He explained what the coins were worth and what they were called, and Kevin divided them.

"To be sure, you can earn more," Uncle Michael said. "I'll not worry, for ye've a good head on your shoulders. Even if 'tis a red one." The O'Hallorans all had black hair.

"What you want to do is go to Newspaper Row, like I did meself when first here," Uncle Michael explained.

"Newspaper Row," Kevin repeated.

" 'Tis really Park Row, but they call it Newspaper Row, see, because all the papers is printed nearby. Get there at daybreak, buy a few copies at each office, and you're in business. Don't buy too many. You can always get more. Selling papers is better than shining shoes, to my way of thinking. You're a freeborn Irishman. You've no need to kneel before any man, nor get your hands caked with blacking.

"Now tell me, how are things in county Limerick?"

By the end of the visit, Kevin felt ready to start earning money. Uncle Michael made New York City sound like a good place to get ahead. Kevin was confident that next time he came to visit, he could give Uncle Michael more money for tobacco and candy and any other comforts the prison allowed.

But seated in the horsecar going downtown, he lost his confidence. He missed his mother sadly. In all this great city he had no friend, not even anyone to talk to until next Sunday, when he could visit Uncle Michael again.

He decided to ride as far as City Hall Park and go and take a look at Newspaper Row.

Dozens of smart carriages were whirling up and down Broadway, and at City Hall Park a great many nicely dressed people were taking Sunday strolls among the flower beds. Did all these people buy newspapers? Kevin's head spun with attempts to calculate the money he could earn. Uncle Michael said each paper made a profit of half a cent. There were more people coming and going than he could count. If half of them bought papers—A person could get rich in no time.

3

Newsboy

It was still dark when Kevin was awakened by the increasing noise in the street. The clip-clop of hooves and the clatter of iron-bound wheels began an unceasing rumble, for wagons transported all the needs of a great city, such as coal and milk and barrels of flour and beer.

Kevin tumbled out of bed. Shivering in the unheated room, he pulled on his jacket but cheerfully left his shoes where they stood. Children here ran about the streets barefoot the same as in Ireland. He put his money in his pocket and crept downstairs to wash his face at the pump. The morning was growing light when he set off for Newspaper Row. He was surprised to see so many people up and about, but they were mostly roughly dressed laborers on their way to work, not men who bought papers.

Printing-House Square was active indeed. Boys big and little were collected around the pressroom door of each newspaper. Delivery vans lined the street, waiting to take the papers to the far parts of town. Some of them carried big advertisements on their sides with the name of the paper they bore. The horses hitched to the vans were blanketed against the early morning chill.

Kevin edged up to one of the lines of waiting boys. A ragged, bright-eyed lad caught sight of him.

"Here's a new one!" he shouted.

All eyes turned. The line was abandoned as boys surrounded Kevin.

"Where'd *you* come from?" half a dozen voices demanded.

Kevin felt his face grow red. He had never been the center of so much attention. Nevertheless he replied stoutly, "County Limerick."

"By gorry!" someone cried. "Another paddy! When did you get off the boat?"

"My name's neither Paddy nor Patrick," Kevin said with dignity. He started to add, "I got off the boat two days ago," but the wave of laughter drowned his words.

"Bless you, we calls all Irishers paddies," whooped a dirty-faced urchin with pale hair hanging below his cap. Kevin remembered the landlady's words: 'The foreman called him "paddy" once too often.'

Kevin clenched his fists and stood ready to defend himself, but a big freckled boy with dark red hair pushed through the crowd.

"Who's talking against the Irish?" he demanded. "Come on, say it to me!"

"Aw, shut up, Pat," grumbled a deep voice. "Nobody's talking against you."

"Oh, yeah?" Pat said. "I thought somebody mentioned me name."

"Your cousin's here from county Limerick," cried the pale-haired youngster, dodging behind another boy.

Pat made a dash at him as if to punish him for his sassiness, but at that moment the double door above the loading dock opened. With a chorus of shouts the boys scrambled back into line. Above their heads a man began handing down papers to one boy after another in exchange for coins. Some of the boys then rushed away, intent on selling them fast and returning for more. Others left in a leisurely fashion, ready to suit themselves to a later-rising public.

Kevin and Pat were left face to face. A shapeless cap topped Pat's red curls at a jaunty angle. His brown eyes appeared to be the same color as the freckles covering his face, arms and as much of his legs as showed below his rolled-up pants. He grinned and stuck out his hand.

"Me name's Patrick Francis Xavier O'Toole. "What's yours?"

"Kevin O'Rourke."

"How long have ye been in New York?" Pat asked.

"Two days."

While they waited their turn at the back doors of the *Sun* and some other papers, Pat explained the customs.

"Some of us big fellows that has a long ways to go to our beats don't wait to buy more than one kind of paper. Some just buys the *Sun* or the *Tribune*, or whatever, but I got regular customers for all the big dailies, so I waits and gets them all, see?

"If I was you," he told Kevin, "I'd start down Nassau Street and find a corner that ain't already took.

Watch out you don't take someone else's beat, that's all. Or you *could* go to South Ferry." He eyed Kevin critically. "How old are you? Nine?"

"Eleven."

"You're small for eleven. We lets the little ones work at South Ferry."

Kevin would have liked to deny that he was small, but it was true. He was small-boned and scrawny. Only his mop of red-orange hair made him stand out in a crowd.

They paid for their papers and withdrew from the clamor.

"Now, let's see what the news is today." Pat began laboriously to work out the headlines: " 'GREELEY'—that's old Horace Greeley, the editor of the *Tribune*. He's running for President, you know—"

" 'GREELEY SAYS EUROPE DOOMED' " Kevin read aloud.

"Can you read that easy?" Pat stared. "Golly! You'll be a natural if you can scream. Here, put your hand to your mouth like this. You got to make your noise carry a long ways. Above the wind, too. Let's hear you scream."

Kevin drew a deep breath and shouted with all

his might: "GREELEY SAYS EUROPE DOOMED!"

Pat shook his head. "Louder!"

Kevin tried again.

Pat nodded reluctantly. "That'll do to begin with. When I gets tired of yelling the headlines, I just shouts, 'Morning papers—Latests news by the steamer.' Sometimes that's better, if the news ain't interesting. Listen, I got to go. See you tomorrow." Pat went off to catch a horsecar that would take him uptown.

Alone and frightened, Kevin walked slowly down the thoroughfare, hoping someone would stop him and demand a paper. The crowds of men and a few women hurrying to work grew thicker, but at every corner a boy was already screaming the headlines.

Kevin turned east towards the river. He didn't want to go to South Ferry with the little kids. At last he found a vacant corner where quite a few men were passing, but he could not bring himself to shout. He stood still, hoping people would see the papers under his arm, but no one paused. He had already learned that Americans despised his Irish accent, and he determined to learn to speak the way they did as soon as possible.

At last he gathered his courage. He took a deep breath, stared into space and raised his voice: "*Morning papers!*"

No one even looked at him. He grew bolder. "Morning papers! Get your morning paper."

To his surprise, a man barked "*Tribune!*" and dropped two pennies into Kevin's hand. Kevin gave him a *Tribune* and stared at the coppers. His first American earnings. With a pleased laugh he shoved them into his pocket.

The sun came up and warmed the street. Kevin grew more confident. He began approaching well-dressed men directly: "Have a paper, sir?" Sometimes they already had one. Sometimes they bought.

He lost his shyness, and for a while he screamed the headlines. Then his voice cracked. He was growing hoarse. Anyway, it was time for breakfast.

Half a block away was a workingman's cafe. Timidly Kevin took a seat at an empty table. He paid three pennies for coffee and a roll. He was taking his first bite when another newsboy flopped into the chair across the table. Kevin recognized the ragged, dark-eyed boy who'd spotted him in the line.

"I saw you at Pine Street," the boy said. "I suppose you know that's Stretch's beat? He'll pound you into the paving when he finds you there."

Kevin had felt frightened ever since he set foot in America, so now he only felt more frightened. He swallowed. Nothing terrible had happened to him yet. He had even made some money.

"Where is he then?" he asked.

The boy shrugged. "Sick, maybe. He was looking kind of peaked."

"When?"

The boy shrugged again. "Since two, three days."

"Maybe he won't come back."

"Maybe he's dead—you wish!" The boy hooted. "You wouldn't get his corner if he was. Some big fellow would take it. That's a good corner, that is."

Kevin swallowed his breakfast hurriedly, deciding to make the most of the corner while he could. The other boy was not unfriendly. His name was Lem. His earnings went to help his mother feed four little sisters. He didn't say where his father was.

Knowing he had a good beat made Kevin try harder. He approached passersby and croaked, "Paper, sir?" until he sold the last one.

Jubilantly he returned to Printing-House Square, jingling the pennies in his pocket. He bought ten copies of the next edition and returned. Business was slow, but by noon he had sold the ten. He bought a boiled egg and a baked potato from a peddler and sat on the curb to eat.

He began to feel lonely again. He wished Pat hadn't gone so far uptown. Even that boy Lem would be company.

The whole day was like that. In the afternoon he bought the evening papers and did a brisk business between five and six o'clock. He treated himself to a hot dinner of boiled meat, potatoes and gravy.

In his room that night he emptied his day's earnings on the bed. At this rate he might have a dollar to take to Uncle Michael next Sunday. He tied the pennies into a corner of his mother's shawl and tucked it under the mattress.

NEXT MORNING City Hall clock was striking six when Kevin arrived at Printing-House Square. He expected to be among the first in line, but a few boys were already sitting against the building. Among them was Pat. He saw Kevin and got up.

"Good morning to you," he said with a grin. "I hear you got Stretch's corner."

"Till he comes back." Kevin felt a burst of gratitude for the bigger boy's friendliness.

"I heard he went West," Pat said.

Kevin's stomach tightened. Was he going to have to fight for the corner? He'd intended to find another spot when Stretch returned, but if Stretch wasn't coming back . . .

"Maybe you'll be lucky," Pat suggested. "Maybe none of the big fellows wants that corner. No one here does, or they'd have said so when we was talking about Stretch."

Kevin smothered a yawn and looked round in bewilderment. The growing light showed more and more boys huddled in the doorways or curled on sidewalk gratings.

"I thought I was early!" Kevin exclaimed.

Pat gave a loud laugh. "Can't nobody be earlier than us! We sleeps here."

"Where?"

"On the sidewalk. Over the gratings, if possible, where the warm air comes out."

"But it's cold!" Kevin's bare feet were far from warm.

"Sure 'tis. But lots of us does it, if we has a bad week or loses our money pitching pennies. Like I did yesterday."

Kevin promised himself that he would never be so foolish as to gamble his money.

THE FIRST WEEK all went pretty well. He had to defend his corner against a big shambling boy whose wild punches Kevin easily ducked. Kevin rattled in and gave him a bloody nose. Later when Lem told him the fellow wasn't very bright, he felt regretful. But after all, he had claimed the beat first.

On Saturday he paid for his room, and on Sunday he took a dollar's worth of dimes to Uncle Michael.

THE SECOND WEEK Pat introduced Kevin to the Bowery Theatre, and Kevin felt that he had found where he belonged. For the price of a dime, the Bowery Theatre gave him what he craved—companionship, excitement, warmth, light, and entertainment. Any night he could join a crowd of newsboys there, most of whom, like himself, had no home to go to. The ground floor in front of the stage was called the pit. They sprawled on the benches there, napping or chattering and eating peanuts until the play began. The sorriest moment of the whole day was when the curtain closed at the end and Kevin and the others had to shuffle out into the dark.

At the end of that week, when Kevin got ready to go to Blackwell's Island on Sunday morning, he found he didn't have enough money to give Uncle Michael the dollar he'd promised and still pay his rent.

Mrs. Riley accepted what he had and agreed to wait until he earned the rest. Monday he had a good day and paid what he owed. Saturday seemed a long way off; it would be easy to catch up.

Tuesday it rained. Not the soft rain of county Limerick, where the water melted into the air, but a pouring rain that people scurried to escape. It soaked into Kevin's papers almost before he reached his corner. He found shelter under a dripping awning, but few people paused to buy a paper. At noon people stayed inside and sent errand boys out to buy lunches. Kevin finally found a dry spot in the entrance of one of the big buildings, but another newsboy was sheltering there, too. They both finally sold all their papers, but it was clearly useless to return for more.

Kevin ate a roll and slouched off toward Baxter Street, jingling the pennies he'd earned. His way led back past Printing-House Square. He had made friends with several other newsboys. He wondered what they were doing this wet afternoon.

The back doors of the printing houses had big awnings over their loading docks to keep the papers dry as they left the building. Here Kevin found his fellows, kicking their heels on the dock, waiting for the rain to stop. Another knot of them was on the sidewalk, pitching pennies. Kevin stopped to watch. Someone offered to teach him the game. Almost before he learned it, he had lost all the spare money in his pockets.

A boy called Gimpy clapped him on the shoulder. "Don't worry, Kevin. There's always tomorrow. Rain can't last forever."

However, it lasted the rest of the week, and the weather turned cold and miserable, so that the only place to escape was the theater. At the end of the week Kevin had no money for room rent.

In a panic he sought Pat.

"So sleep on the street, like we does," Pat said with a shrug and a laugh. "It's cheaper."

"What about my things?"

"Maybe Mrs. Riley will keep 'em for you. Or leave 'em with your uncle. They'll be safe there!" Pat roared at his own joke. "What do you have?"

"My mother's dress, her shawl, a blanket . . . my shoes."

"Sell 'em," Pat advised. "Maybe give the money to your uncle, if you're short this week."

"What about the prayerbook and her marriage paper?"

"Well, *her* marriage paper ain't no good to *you* The prayerbook—maybe give it to a priest?"

They disposed of the clothes at a secondhand store, but when they tried to give away the prayerbook, the jolly-faced priest frowned. He demanded to know how long since the boys had been to confession. He then ordered Kevin to keep the book and use it.

In the end Kevin left it and the hand mirror with Mrs. Riley. He treated Pat to a hot meal with the money from the sale of the clothes.

After the theater that evening, Pat showed him how to steal into the *Sun* building through the door the printers used. Once inside Pat led him stealthily to the lobby. There in the darkness Kevin made out half a dozen forms, snuggled together like puppies. Pat and Kevin crept in among them.

The tile floor was not much harder than the ship's bunk. The big presses in the basement set up a noise and a trembling that was as good as a lullaby. The presses were rolling tonight that Kevin might earn money tomorrow. Before they lulled him to sleep, he thought over his career. He had been in America three weeks. He had found a livelihood, a place to spend his evenings and a free roof. Pretty good! The newsboys considered themselves a fast set, and Kevin was proud to be one of them.

4

The Newsboys' Lodging House

Kevin settled contentedly into this free and easy life. November came with its early darkness, but the weather stayed warm. The newspapers began forecasting an easy winter. However, there were frequent rainy days when falling leaves stuck to wet pavement and papers were hard to sell. Kevin often rejoiced that he had no rent to pay. He continued to visit Uncle Michael, but Baxter Street saw him no more. He preferred the bustle and excitement of Printing-House Square. If no better entertainment offered, one could slip into the vast cellars and watch the presses run. They gobbled white sheets of newsprint and spat them out covered with lines of type.

He became acquainted with the people who passed his corner every morning and acquired some regular customers. His bright hair made passersby remember him. His was a cheery face on the street of hurrying, drab-clothed workers.

He was industrious, too. As soon as he sold the morning's armload of papers, he rushed back to Printing-House Square to await the next edition. While waiting, he breakfasted on a roll and coffee and pitched pennies or rolled dice with the other newsboys. He was popular; he could read the headlines and be trusted to read them right. The printers liked to trick boys who couldn't read. They would send some unlettered lad into the street shouting, "QUEEN VICTORIA REMARRIED" or "CALIFORNIA DECLARES WAR."

Kevin was now earning about three dollars a week, but except for the dollar he gave Uncle Michael, the pennies never stayed long in his pocket. What he didn't spend on food and the theater, he lost at gambling. He seldom won, but it didn't matter; there was always tomorrow's edition.

He washed his face and feet at a hydrant by City Hall Park. When his shirt got too dirty to wear, he threw it away and bought one from a secondhand store. He considered that he knew his way about. Even the bigger boys liked him, perhaps because he never complained about his gambling losses.

"Come on," Pat said one evening in late November. "There's a new show at the Bowery."

Heavy clouds had drizzled all day. Now that the rain had stopped, a cold wind was blowing. However the boys' pants and jackets, though threadbare, were wool and warm even when damp. They ran all the way to the theater and arrived breathless and tingling.

The show was called *Buffalo Bill, The King of the Border Men*. Afterwards every boy in the pit agreed it was the best show the Bowery had ever had.

Pat and Kevin headed for their bedroom in the *Sun* lobby, discussing the play.

"My eyes, wouldn't I like to be out West!" Pat exclaimed. "Huntin' buffalo and gold. Or driving a stagecoach! Can't you just see me. Hup! You blithering, crosseyed mules! Giddap!" He cursed the imaginary animals and tore off down the quiet street, firing a make-believe shotgun at make-believe Indians.

No printers were at the side door, and the boys made their way into the building without being seen. By now Kevin knew the turns and hallways as well as though he'd seen them by daylight, which he never had. The sleepers there crept out again before the janitors came.

Word of the warm, dry lobby had spread, and the number of homeless boys it housed had increased as nights grew colder. On this particular night others drifted in from the theater until fifteen or twenty huddled there.

Kevin made himself comfortable. Pat curled up against his back.

Moments later, it seemed, Kevin was roused by light flashing in his eyes, the sound of a splash, and cries. *Hey! Oh, you dirty—! Cut it out!* Another splash and the deep-voiced laughter of men.

Awake on the instant, Kevin saw three printers in the doorway, holding buckets. The huddle of bodies on the floor was dissolving into individual boys who ducked past the printers and fled down the hallway.

"Hey, Charlie!" a man shouted. "Give us another bucketful. Two! Good! That ought to do it."

Before Kevin could get to his feet, cold water sluiced over him. He ran for the hallway and heard another bucketful splash onto the boys behind him. He heard Pat cursing as he ran.

They stood on the sidewalk, shivering and dripping. The nearest clock tower said one-thirty. Some of the smaller boys were crying.

"Mean, mean, mean!" Pat raged. "We wasn't doing no harm! I know who they was, too. Wait till I get one of them alone!" He made ferocious jabs at the air.

"We should have gone to the lodge," someone nearby wailed. "I told you we should have!"

"What's that?" Kevin raised his voice. "What's the lodge?"

"The Newsboys' Lodging House, paddy." A voice spoke from the dark. "Don't you even know that?"

Kevin promised himself he'd find out. Meanwhile, he and Pat and an urchin named Oscar had to find some place to sleep. A fight had already started for space on the sidewalk grating, where warm air drifted up from the pressrooms.

"I know a place under a stairway," Pat said. "It ain't great, but no one's going to run us out."

"Do you know what the Newsboys' Lodging House is?" Kevin asked as they set out.

"It's a Sunday school racket," Pat said.

"What do you mean?"

"This society runs it. It ain't exactly a Sunday school, but you can't chew tobacco or swear, and it costs six cents for a bed."

"Have you been there?"

"No. It's been warm enough to sleep out since I been on me own. I'd rather spend me money on *Buffalo Bill*."

"I don't chew tobacco and I don't swear," Oscar piped.

"Yes, and you ain't got six cents, either," Pat said crossly.

Cramped under the stairway, with the cold creeping from his feet to his legs, Kevin thought he would rather have a warm bed than the theater. If he quit gambling, he could have both.

Somehow, despite the cold and their wet garments, the boys dozed until rumbling delivery wagons told them it was time to line up for papers.

"Soon's we get 'em," Pat said through chattering teeth, "let's get a cup of coffee. I'll treat yous if you're broke."

While they waited in line, they asked about the lodging house. Pat had decided to try it, too.

"Middle of the block on Park Place," they were told.

"They don't take Irishers, though!" teased one of the big boys.

"If they takes riffraff like you, I don't know as I want to go there!" Pat cried, squaring up to the heckler, who was half a head taller. "It's probably got bedbugs."

"No, it ain't!" squealed a little boy. "There's *showers* and all the soap you want. And for six cents more they gives you supper."

"Supper of what?" Pat asked suspiciously.

"Pork and beans! All you can eat. They don't care if you're Irish or not."

Pat laughed. "I'll bet they do! I'll bet they says to themselves, 'Lucky us, we got two Irishmen tonight!' "

LATE THAT AFTERNOON Kevin met up with Pat and Oscar. They went timidly through the doors of the Newsboys' Lodging House, but upon seeing three boys seated on a bench, Pat resumed his swagger.

The boys were newcomers like themselves. "You have to wait here," one said. "Get on line. That man in there has to talk to you."

"What about?" Pat asked.

"I don't know."

They took places on the bench, swinging their feet and talking about the day's business.

Kevin studied the framed mottoes adorning the walls.

Oscar nudged him. "What do they say?"

"That one says, SHALL THERE BE A GOD TO SWEAR BY AND NONE TO PRAY TO?"

"What's it mean?" Oscar asked.

Pat leaned across Kevin to answer. "It means it's a Sunday school racket, like I said."

Kevin frowned him to silence. "The one beside the door says, A BOY'S BEST FRIEND IS A GOOD EDUCATION; COME REGULARLY TO EVENING SCHOOL. Hey, I might look into that."

"Give up the theater!" Pat exclaimed.

"A person doesn't have to go every night! You should learn to read, Pat. That sign there says, BOYS WHO ARE IN TROUBLE OR IN WANT OF HOMES AND EMPLOYMENT WILL FIND THE SUPERINTENDENT WILLING TO HELP THEM. But how do you know, if you can't read?"

"I has my secretary read it," Pat said with a lordly air.

Kevin sniffed. "That one," he told Oscar, says WISE BOYS PUT THEIR PENNIES IN THE SAVINGS BANK

AND GET FIVE PERCENT A MONTH INTEREST."

"What's interest?" Oscar asked. Neither Pat nor Kevin could tell him.

Pat's turn to see the superintendent came first. When he came out, he headed for the stairs. "I'll pick three beds together," he shouted and was gone.

Oscar went next. "Your turn," he told Kevin when he came out.

"What did he say to you?"

"He asked me how old I am and why I don't have a home. He patted me on the head and said the people here would help me. Want me to wait?"

"No, go find Pat." Kevin went in to talk to the superintendent.

The man behind the desk looked like a school-teacher. When Kevin gave him his name, he said, "Well, Kevin, how do you happen to come here?" His questions were kindly. Kevin found himself telling everything that had happened since he left Ireland.

"Do you like this sort of life?"

Kevin groped for an answer. "I guess I don't have any choice, sir."

"We might be able to offer you a choice."

"I'd like to go to school some more, sir," Kevin confided. "I like to read."

The man nodded. "Go up now and take a shower and look around. I hope you'll stay here every night. In a month or two maybe we can offer you something better," he added mysteriously.

Kevin found Pat and Oscar. Pat had already learned his way around. He showed them the dining room, the schoolroom, gymnasium and shower room, and two upper stories of iron bunks.

Supper was, as promised, all they could eat of pork and beans. Afterwards Pat and Oscar went off to the theater; the doors of the lodging house did not close until eleven thirty.

Kevin chose to attend the evening class. He had again become careful of money. He hadn't gone to visit Uncle Michael last Sunday because he hadn't had a dollar to give him. This Sunday he was going to make up for it.

About twenty boys straggled into the classroom. The teacher was dressed in a smart suit and polished boots. Kevin learned he was a banker who spent one evening a week teaching boys to read. When he discovered Kevin could already read well, he settled him in a corner with a book called *Twenty Thousand Leagues Under the Sea*.

At the end of two hours Kevin reluctantly gave

back the book. He would have liked to go on reading, but the class was over. He climbed the stairs to where the bunks were, hung his pants and jacket on the nails provided, and crept between the cotton blankets. He pulled the thick comforter up to his chin and sighed.

Boys continued to come in. Kevin tried to stay awake to enjoy his bed's cozy warmth and wait for Pat. He was drifting off when he heard Pat's whisper, "Kevin, you awake?"

"Yes."

"You know what puzzles me?"

"No," Kevin murmured.

"How come there ain't *more* boys? How come this place ain't overflowing with boys? It's too good to be true, that's why! How come they're doing this for us?"

5

"Go West, Young Man"

At the end of the week, Kevin found out why the lodging house wasn't overflowing. He had come in early. The first snowflakes of the season were plopping wetly on newspapers and sidewalks alike. He found the lobby humming with excitement. A group of boys, most of whom he had come to know through seeing them at meals, were standing about in overcoats and new mittens.

Another boy, also dressed for travel, came rushing in from the sidewalk. "The carriages is here!" he shouted.

Away marched the superintendent, the boys, and a man Kevin had never seen before.

An urchin known as Shorty was standing nearby.

"What's going on?" Kevin asked.

"They's off to catch the night boat to Albany."

"What for?"

"What for! They's going *West!*"

"How come?"

"The lodge is sending them West. Crikey, I wisht I could go, but I'd never get to see my mother then. Now I sees her on her day off."

So many questions bounded into Kevin's mind he couldn't sort them out fast enough to speak.

"Why?" he stammered at last.

"Why what?"

"Why are they sending them away?"

" 'Cause they wants to get them off the streets, and people out West wants boys."

The superintendent came back inside, brushing snow from his coat. His eye fell on Kevin. He said, "Come into my office, O'Rourke. I want to talk to you."

Kevin followed him into the room, wondering what he'd done wrong, but the superintendent said,

"Sit down," and offered him licorice. "Did you see those boys leaving, Kevin? We're sending them to Michigan, to people who want to give them homes. The older ones will probably go to work for farmers. They'll get board and wages. The younger ones will go to people who want to take a boy and raise him. I was thinking that might be a chance for you to get more schooling. Are you free to leave New York? I think you told me your parents have both passed away."

Kevin's head was spinning. To go West! What was it really like out there? It sounded like the most marvelous adventure in the world. What boy, after seeing Buffalo Bill's Wild West show, wouldn't want to go West? But he was forgetting Uncle Michael.

"My uncle's at Blackwell's Island, sir," he told the superintendent. "I don't know as I could go off and leave him."

"Why don't you talk it over. See what he says. We won't send another group out till after Christmas."

"Would they be going to Michigan, sir?" Perhaps Uncle Michael would like to leave New York when he came out of prison.

The superintendent consulted a paper. "The next group is going to Nebraska. You think about it."

KEVIN WENT to Blackwell's Island that Sunday, as planned. First he told Uncle Michael all about the Newsboys' Lodging House, and at last, that the people who ran it wanted to send him to Nebraska.

Uncle Michael's eyes narrowed. "And what would ye be doin' out there with them wild Indians?"

"There's people out there who wants boys."

"What do they want them for, did the superintendent tell you that?"

"To work, I guess. But they send them to school, too."

"And who is doin' this good deed?"

"It's called the Children's Aid Society."

"Charity!" Uncle Michael turned up his snub nose. His thick black hair had been growing all these weeks, and he looked more like himself. "I don't know whether your mother would approve of that. I'll ask around here, me boy, and see what I find out."

"Could you ask now?"

"You're wanting to go, are ye? You've set your heart on it."

Kevin allowed himself a brief nod. He had just

realized how much.

"I could write you every week," he offered. "It ain't as good as visiting, but you could get someone to read it—"

"I can read it meself!" Uncle Michael bragged. "If you write a good hand. They've taught me to read here, Kevin. You *could* say I've profited by my time."

"That's wonderful, Uncle Michael!" Kevin exclaimed. "Maybe you could even come there when you get out."

"Not so fast, me boy. I haven't said you could go yet. You come back next week, after I've thought it over. How do you know anybody will want ye when ye get there?

"Ah, you don't know!" he said when Kevin shook his head. "You ask those charitable gents the answer to that one."

Kevin said he would. He realized, too, that once he went out West, Uncle Michael wouldn't get any pocket money.

I'll save up all my extra money between now and when I go, he promised himself. *If* I go. I won't hardly even go to the theater. I'll give it all to Uncle Michael before I leave.

The following Sunday Kevin's heart beat faster

as the boat approached the prison. He had thought of nothing but the West all week. The superintendent had even read letters one night at dinner that the society had received from boys who'd already gone. He said he wanted them to think seriously about leaving their life on the streets before they were pressed to become members of the gangs—the tough Dead Rabbits, or the Plug Uglies. One letter from a seventeen-year-old made its hearers titter. The boy wrote: "I had to leave my place because Mr. Harmon prayed too much at home and swore too much in the cornfield. I don't like that sort of man."

"So you see," the superintendent said, "you'll be as free to make your own way out there as you are here. And the opportunities are vastly greater."

Another older boy wrote: "When I first came to Kansas I did not know a single person, but the next day I got a job as driver of the mail. I stayed at that for five months, then having passed an examination, I received a teacher's certificate. I have now taught two months with success. I am glad of the opportunity I now have of being useful to my fellow men."

The boys didn't think much of someone who would give up driving the U.S. mail to teach school. They had looked at Nebraska on the map, and Kevin had scanned every day's paper for news about it. And one day the papers had reported that railroad tracks had been laid across more miles of prairie.

When at last Kevin stood before Uncle Michael's cell, he could not bring himself to ask the question. They talked about everything under the sun before his uncle said at last, "Are ye still wantin' to go West, Kevin?"

Kevin's throat felt tight. He could only nod.

"I'm thinkin' 'tis the thing for ye to do," Uncle Michael said.

Kevin felt limp with relief. He would tell the superintendent as soon as he could get back to the lodging house.

Uncle Michael scratched himself. "Blast the lice here!" he exclaimed. "Did you find out what's to become of you out there if nobody wants you?"

"The superintendent says it never happens. They put up notices in the town, and people apply to a committee. Most times the committee is a preacher and maybe the mayor."

"And do you know the town?"

"It's called Cottonwood City. The superintendent says a cottonwood is a tree."

"It's what your blessed mother and father wanted

for ye—a better life. One of us must find something good here. I'm thinking it will be you. I'll join you if ever I get my freedom."

"Did you ask anyone about the society?" Kevin inquired.

Uncle Michael said, "I asked one of the guards, one of the higher-ups. He'd heard of it. He said anything to get you away from the streets would be a good thing. To which I agreed."

"We won't go till after Christmas," Kevin bubbled. "The superintendent says January. I'll give you all the extra money I earn between now and then. That ought to last a while."

"Of course it will," Uncle Michael agreed. "Don't you worry about me, young Kevin. You take care of yourself. The city's taking fine care of me. But make sure you write, so we won't lose track of one another."

Kevin promised he would.

"A rich woman is paying our train fares, and the girls at the Girls' Lodging House are knitting us mittens and caps."

"Maybe a kindhearted colleen would knit me a cap," his uncle suggested.

Kevin did not approve of joking about girls.

"We never see them," he said. "They just do it. And the rich woman is going to give us warm coats and underwear, too. Everything we need."

"Maybe you could recommend me to *her*." Uncle Michael laughed.

"I don't think we'll ever see her, either," Kevin told him. "Unless at Christmas. You know what we're having for Christmas? Turkey dinner! And a party. Maybe even Santa Claus. For the little boys. And then, two weeks after Christmas we leave. My friend Pat won't go, even though the superintendent says it's the best thing that could happen."

"My prayers go with ye," Uncle Michael said.

Kevin nodded his thanks. But he thought Uncle Michael could use some prayers for himself.

6

The Long Journey

he weather was warm in December. It rained, but no more snow fell, and Kevin gave no thought to his shoeless condition. All the younger newsboys were barefoot. They were inured to cold feet and chilblains and stubbed toes. Once a week he went to the theater; the rest of his money he saved for Uncle Michael.

Christmas came, marked by the promised turkey dinner and party. Santa Claus and Mrs. Santa handed out a bagful of clothing. Kevin got a red flannel undershirt, scratchy but warm.

On New Year's Day the Superintendent announced that the next group for the West would go a week from Tuesday. Only three boys besides Kevin had applied. He paid his last visit to Uncle Michael, gave him the pocket money he'd saved, and promised to write.

When the day came, Kevin did not waste the morning. He went out and sold his papers as usual. "Because it's good to have money in your pocket," he said to himself.

That afternoon the intending travellers lined up in the lobby of the lodging house. Everything they owned was on their backs or in their pockets. Everyone was wearing the promised caps and mittens; and new coats and shoes had been supplied by the society to keep them warm on the trip and on the icy plains of Nebraska. They were too excited to stand still, but Kevin remembered to keep his eye on the hampers of food he was in charge of.

A sprinkling of youngsters gathered to see them off, looking envious, though they hadn't had the courage to go. Pat self-consciously said goodbye and hurried away, as if fearing he might be tempted.

The agent arrived to take them in charge—a thin, gray-haired man with a white moustache and deepset eyes. He was shepherding a three-year-old. The child had a cruel purple bruise across one thin cheek. He was bundled into an outsize coat that came nearly to his shoetops. His ankles looked like matchsticks.

"This is Peter. His mother abandoned him on the ferry this morning," the agent told the superintendent. "It was either the West or the Foundling Home. I said we'd take him. The girls can look after him."

"Girls!" The whisper went round the room.

The agent turned to the waiting boys. "Yes, four girls are joining our group."

"This is Mr. Carter," the superintendent said, and began introducing the boys.

George and Kevin were the same age, but no one would have guessed it. George was a head taller than Kevin and as sturdy as a Shetland pony. Hiram, twelve, and James, thirteen, though skinny, were well-grown. They all knew each other, having spent entire evenings talking about the adventurous life out West—Indians, cowboys, lucky strikes of gold and silver.

Boys, hampers, and Mr. Carter squeezed into a hackney cab. Everyone staying behind shouted goodbye, and they were off. They were to take the night boat to Albany and there board an emigrant train.

In the ladies' waiting room at the pier, a woman turned the girls over to Mr. Carter: four white-faced, tough-looking, underfed street waifs: Hannah, ten; Elizabeth, eight; Maggie, seven; and Dolly, five.

"What're *they* going to do out West?" Hiram muttered. "They don't need girls there."

The woman heard this. "Girls *are* needed," she said, "to bring a softening touch to those rough communities." Behind her, Elizabeth stuck out her tongue and called Hiram a dirty name.

The biggest girl, Hannah, retied Peter's shoelaces and led him off to the toilet.

"Elizabeth, you will be responsible for Dolly," the woman said. As soon as she turned away, Elizabeth stuck out her tongue at *her*.

Kevin liked Hannah. She reminded him of Mary Finn, his friend aboard ship.

They boarded the boat and raced to explore it. When it began to move away from the pier, however, they gathered around Mr. Carter and Peter, who was too small to be turned loose.

"Three cheers for New York!" George cried. They cheered lustily, though not one of them was sorry to be leaving.

"Three cheers for Nebraska!" shouted Hiram.

They responded so enthusiastically that a man who worked on the boat ordered them down to steerage where they belonged. As soon as he disappeared, they bounced upstairs again, but the January evening was too cold to stay outside. Darkness descended over the river, and they went back downstairs where it was warm. Mr. Carter opened a hamper and brought out cheese and crackers, followed by gingerbread. After trips to the washrooms, they settled themselves for the night. The boat was not crowded, so there was room to stretch out on the benches.

At daybreak the boat tied up at Albany. Mr. Carter led his shivering charges to a waterfront cafe and ordered bowls of steaming oatmeal and cups of coffee. Little Peter had to be coaxed to drink milk; he, too, had learned to drink coffee.

"Mister, who's paying for this?" James asked. Ears perked up around the table. They had all been wondering. Every one of them had learned that food costs money.

"A rich New York man," Mr. Carter said.

"Why?"

"Both he and the society think you'll have a better life out West."

"Does he pay you for taking us?" James asked shrewdly.

"Yes. This is the way I make my living."

The boys' eyes widened, and they looked at each other.

"I'd like a job like that!" James said.

The rest agreed. They couldn't understand why Mr. Carter laughed. "Let's see whether you still think so at the end of the trip," he said.

At the railroad depot the little band worked their way through the chattering crowd of what seemed hundreds of emigrants all heading West—Germans, Irish, Italians, Norwegians. When the train doors opened, the mass rushed in. By the time the children got into a car, it was nearly full—people standing, sitting on laps and on bundles, a good many on the floor.

"Dear me!" Mr. Carter exclaimed. "Let's hope a great many of these people will get off in New York state."

The car throbbed with the babble of voices. For many of the passengers this was the last part of a longer journey. They had already traveled, first by train and then by boat, to reach America. Now they were filled with hope and excitement.

It was noon before the train started and the long ride began. The Irishmen passed around whiskey and sang. German men and woman smoked and sang. Babies squalled and were nursed.

There being nothing shy about Kevin's group, most of them managed to squeeze up to a window. Some had never seen the country before. Their newsboy voices soared over the din.

"Oh! Oh! Look at the snow! This must be the North Pole. Look at them skaters! And the sleds—!"

"What's that, Mister Carter?"

"A corn field. Those are corn shocks."

"Oh, yeah! Them's what makes buckwheaters."

"Look at them cows! My mother used to milk cows."

By the end of the afternoon, Kevin, George, and Hiram were squeezed into one seat, with Peter sleeping across their laps. Mr. Carter, Hannah and Elizabeth shared the seat facing them, and Mr. Carter held Maggie. James found himself a place on the floor at the end of the car. Dolly refused to sit on Hannah's lap. She crept under the seat, where she napped on Mr. Carter's coat. Luckily they got settled before dark because the car's lamps were out of oil. Mr.

Carter passed around the last of the gingerbread and cheese, and they slept.

At Rochester next morning the train stopped for an hour to give the emigrants time to eat breakfast and use the washrooms. Mr. Carter settled his charges in the railroad dining room. "We're going to have hot breakfasts along the way," he told them, "so eat all you can. Dinner and supper will have to be bread and cheese and sausage." He hurried away to find a store and a bakery. The city youngsters secured the busy waiter's attention and were being served plates of beefsteak and potatoes by the time Mr. Carter returned. After breakfast the train chugged on.

At the long stops while the train took on coal, most of the Americans would pile out and walk up and down the station platform for exercise. They were curious about nine children travelling together and questioned them. In that way Kevin heard Hannah's story.

"My mother's dead," she told a ring of adults. "My father got his leg cut off in the War. He used his government money to buy drink. When he was drunk, he beat us—me and my stepmothers. I had a lot of stepmothers. They didn't stay long because my father was so mean. I earned money as a ragpicker, but one day when I didn't earn anything, he threw me out. A lady told me about the Girls' Lodging House. I went there, and they taught me housekeeping. Now I'm going West to work for some family and go to school."

Night came again, and still the train chugged westward. Every time it stopped to take on water, Kevin seemed to hear Elizabeth asking peevishly, "Ain't we there *yet?*" And Mr. Carter saying soothingly, "Not yet. Go back to sleep."

The car grew cold as the night wore on, though the men passengers took turns putting more coal into the potbellied stove.

At last the sky grew pale. It was gray and wintry when they pulled into Chicago, and snow began falling as they left the station. Mr. Carter bundled them into a carriage, and they set out for the Burlington Railroad Station. After breakfast they boarded another train.

Again seats were filled with families and baggage, but now the coal stoves at each end of the car were for cooking as well as heating. A group of foreign emigrants had a new trick. Their children old enough to walk had tin plates and cups tied round their necks and hanging down their backs. The New

York urchins laughed at this, but Mr. Carter thought it a good idea and jokingly suggested tying a cup to Peter. But his youngsters were inclined to think themselves superior.

"All these foreigners," Elizabeth said, looking down her nose. "They can't even talk English."

"These are fine people, going West to make a new life, just as you are," Mr. Carter told the group. "Some of you may even get homes with people who don't speak English well. I hope you will help them learn."

"Can *anyone* get a free farm?" James asked.

"These people from the Old Country are buying land from the railroads, but anyone who's twenty-one and a citizen of the United States can stake a claim for a homestead."

"Not girls!" George scoffed.

"Young ladies, too. Anyone who is over twenty-one or head of a family."

"How much can you get?" James asked. The other boys looked at him enviously because he was was nearest twenty-one.

"Depends on where you go," Mr. Carter said. "Eighty acres if you locate near a railroad, a hundred and sixty if you don't mind going farther from neighbors. You file your claim at the land office. Then you go back and build a house and start plowing. You have to live there for five years before the land becomes legally yours. Many people can't stick it out. Those who do must be admired. It takes money, too, because crops can fail."

"That's for me," Hiram said. "As soon as I get to be twenty-one. If there's any land left," he added gloomily after multiplying all the people in that trainload by trainloads each week.

"Get married and do it sooner!" George suggested.

Hiram cuffed him. Mr. Carter's firm voice ordered them to wait till the next station to do their fighting.

Everyone except Mr. Carter was getting short-tempered and cranky. Maggie slapped Dolly, Dolly hit back and both of them burst into tears. And not just their group, either. A fight broke out at one end of the car over a bottle of whiskey. Soon after, a quarrel began in two languages at the other end among people waiting in line to do their cooking.

When the sun came out, sparkling on level, empty fields, everyone became more cheerful. After all, a train trip like this was something that happened only once in a lifetime, and for the most part they were enjoying a holiday.

All day the train rolled across flat land. The country grew more untamed.

"You notice—there are no fences out here?" Hiram said, taking his turn at the window.

Instead of fields full of cornshocks, the snowy countryside looked as though it had never been plowed or planted. Once they glimpsed a boy on a horse, herding cattle. The boys hoped that horseback riding and cow herding would be part of their farm jobs. George was sure he would know instantly how to ride. He would leap into the saddle and be off at a gallop.

"I'd like mine to be all shiny black," Hannah said. "I'd call him Midnight."

"Girls don't ride horses," George told her pityingly. "Only cowboys do that."

"Girls do so!" Elizabeth shouted. "There was a girl on that horse yesterday."

"Her brother was riding it. She was just sitting behind."

"*She* was riding. He was sitting in front of her!"

"That wasn't a horse," Hiram said. "That was a pony."

"I'm going to have a little pony," Elizabeth stated. "And only I can ride it."

"Hooh!" the boys shouted.

Another lively quarrel would have followed, but Mr. Carter began handing out hunks of bread and sausage. It was hard to shout insults with one's mouth full.

That evening they crossed the Mississippi River. Everyone crowded to the windows or stretched their necks to see the endless white landscape give place to muddy water. On the other side was Burlington, Iowa.

At the station the passengers piled out. Some ate a hurried meal in the restaurant, some scurried to the nearest grocery store. Night fell before the train started again.

"I'm tired of riding this train," Maggie whined.

Mr. Carter moved Dolly to one knee and set Maggie on the other. "Tomorrow we'll be in Nebraska," he promised.

Next morning they crossed the Missouri River and puffed into Omaha. A lot of passengers got off there to stay in the railroad's Emigrant Home while they looked for land for sale. The train stayed in Omaha all morning.

"We're going to be about ten hours late," a trainman told Mr. Carter as they got underway at last. "We've got trouble on the line further out." Because of that they would reach their destination in the middle of the night.

The train crawled and so did the hours, but at last the long afternoon came to an end. As it grew dark, Kevin stayed sharply awake, but that didn't make the miles go faster. He closed his eyes.

The next thing he knew, the train had stopped. A trainman holding a lantern was standing in the aisle.

"Cottonwood City, folks."

By the light of the lantern they made their way out onto the platform. The orphans were the only ones getting off. Frozen boards squeaked under their feet. Maggie, Dolly and Peter began to whimper as cold wind slapped their faces.

Inside the railroad depot another lantern glowed. Carrying Peter, Mr. Carter led the way toward it, and the children gathered around the stove.

The station master followed them in, setting his lantern on a shelf and rubbing his hands. "So you're the folks from back East," he said, unwinding the muffler from his head. "This town ain't talked about nothing else since the notice was put up. See that pile of buffalo robes? The young'uns can bed down here till morning."

The girls spread their buffalo hides on one side of the room, and the boys spread theirs on the other. Mr. Carter piled more robes over them, hairy side down.

The furry rugs smelled greasy and dusty. Drifting off Kevin seemed again to be racketing along in the train, but he was warm, hot even, because the train was stuffed with buffalo skins . . .

7

The Choosing

The next thing Kevin knew, Elizabeth was screeching, "Be we there, Mister? Is this Nebraska?"

He threw back the buffalo robe to see sun streaming through the depot window. Elizabeth, George and Maggie were crowding out the door. He heard them running on the platform.

Kevin tied his shoes, fumbling in his haste. Then he, too, was flying out the door.

The countryside was so flat that the station platform felt like a hilltop. Shining steel rails cut across the prairie in both directions. Away over some fields Kevin saw a scattering of one- and two-story buildings. Everywhere else snowy wastelands spread to the horizon, except for one line of bare trees.

George was looking bewildered. "Where's Cottonwood City?"

Kevin, used to the villages of Ireland, said, "That's it."

Hiram came running at them.

"That's not a city! There's more of us than there is houses!" Which wasn't really true.

"Come on!" Kevin set off at top speed toward some clumps of tall weedstalks surrounding snow-covered piles of lumber. The three boys ran past Maggie and Elizabeth, who were galloping round and round a shock of corn in the nearest field. Maggie stopped suddenly. She picked up an ear that had fallen to the ground. Yellow corn peeked from beneath the pale, dried husk.

"Look at this!" She ran shrieking to Mr. Carter.

Elizabeth found the winter remains of a patch of prairie roses. "Berries!" she screeched. The red-orange rose hips did indeed look like fruit. She bit one. Her face scrunched, and she spat.

"Breakfast!" Mr. Carter called from the platform. "Whoever wants breakfast, come along!" Hannah, Mr. Carter and Peter set out along the road to town. The others straggled after, running from side to side, making tracks in the unmarked snow.

The hotel, which was the largest building in town, was beginning to stir when the group trailed across the porch. A man opened the door, exclaiming, "Land alive, these must be the orphans! Molly!" he called over his shoulder. "Breakfast customers!" He directed them to a hallway where they hung their coats. A bench held two big washpans and a bucket of water. A big girl came from the kitchen with a steaming kettle and poured hot water into the basins. Beside the bench hung a long strip of toweling. A mirror was nailed beside it. Hands and faces were washed; Hannah combed the girls' hair and Peter's, and the comb was passed among the rest of the boys. From the neck up, they looked respectable, Kevin thought. The boys had had barber's haircuts before leaving New York. Their clothes, however, were a different story—wrinkled, dirty and even torn, having been lived in for so many days and nights.

They sat on either side of a long, bare table. Pitchers of milk and coffee came from the kitchen, followed by platters of buckwheat cakes and sausage, with sorghum syrup to pour over. There was a pitcher of cream for the coffee and molded hills of butter to spread on the pancakes. After all that, Molly brought out dried apple pies.

Some of the town's bachelors boarded at the hotel. One by one men drifted in, sat at the long table and stared at the children while they cut through stacks of pancakes. They were bearded and booted. Kevin wished his new shoes had been boots.

When the youngsters had eaten all they could hold, Mr. Carter inquired the way to the church, and they filed into the main street, which was wide and rutted and ran east to west like the railroad track. Whichever way Kevin looked, he could see open prairie beyond the houses.

"How can they call this a city?" he whispered to Mr. Carter.

"They're hoping lots of people will move here and make it one."

Despite the cold and the early hour, saddle horses were tied to hitching rails along the street. Men stood gossiping in twos and threes on the board sidewalks, and families drove past in wagons.

Everyone stared. Mr. Carter led the children into the church. Everywhere they heard whispering: "There's the orphans!" "—little, ain't he? They must not have any food in New York City."

The preacher, wearing a black suit, welcomed them. He shook hands with Mr. Carter and sent them all to the empty second row. The first row was full of small, pale-haired children who eyed them over the back of the pew. One pointed at Kevin's hair, and they all giggled.

Kevin's breakfast was now a lump in his stomach as big as a washtub. Maggie had thrown hers up. Peter's bruises still showed, and Dolly looked ready to cry.

Could anybody possibly want any of us, Kevin wondered. James and Hiram were acting too smart for their britches, as if they didn't care whether anyone wanted them or not.

The children had to sit through Sunday school and then church. It passed in a blur. Everyone but Peter knew they were being inspected. The actual choosing would be that afternoon at the courthouse, which was to be opened even though it was Sunday.

After church Mr. Carter took his group back to the hotel. The owner had offered them a free meal, but no one did justice to it, partly due to the mammoth breakfast, but mostly to the ordeal ahead. The dining room seemed full of silent, staring faces. Used to loud city voices, the children found these quiet people frightening. No one had any desire to explore. They waited docilely for what would happen.

The courthouse was one big room. It stood in the corner of an empty square. "The building's only temporary," the preacher apologized as they trailed toward it. "We plan to build a fine stone one. Everything's booming; taxpayers, churchgoers moving in so fast a person can't keep count."

"How are the schools?" Mr. Carter asked.

The preacher beamed. "We have a fine one here in town—fifteen pupils. In the country . . . well, each township does the best it can. Have to educate the young, you know. They're the most important crop the prairie produces, after all." He smiled.

The youngsters stared back amazed. George's mouth actually dropped open, and Hiram nudged James. Never had any of them, except Kevin, been considered anything but a nuisance, an extra mouth to feed.

A crowd was standing about the door, so Kevin was not surprised to see that inside the room was full and men were lining the wall. If *this* many people wanted children . . . perhaps they did have a chance.

The orphans were led to two railed-off benches

at the front of the room. The preacher stepped to the platform.

"Ladies and gentlemen," he began. "We are happy to see so many faces this crisp and sunny afternoon." And he began to tell them how wonderful their community was. Kevin heard guffaws from the back row at some of the more extravagant praise. When he said that southern Nebraska was on the same world parallel as Italy, some wag said, "You sure you don't mean Switzerland, mister?" People chuckled, because everyone knew that Italy was warm and sunny and Switzerland was full of ice and snow. But in general his listeners seemed to enjoy being told about their wonderful choice of a home. He was loudly clapped, after which he introduced Mr. Carter.

Mr. Carter told his audience that thousands of homeless children roamed the streets of New York City. He explained that the Children's Aid Society worked to move them into the country where they could grow into useful men and women instead of beggars and criminals. "These are not young criminals or paupers," he said. "They are simply homeless, unfortunate boys and girls. They are the best material, folks, that a farmer or a master could desire to make into good workers on the farm or in the house."

"How about the little 'uns, mister?" the same voice called. "What's they good for?"

There was some good-natured laughter, but Dolly threw her head into Hannah's lap and began to cry.

Mr. Carter glanced toward her and then said with dignity, "They are good for loving. As our Saviour said, 'Even as you do it unto the least of these, you do it unto me.' I know there are warmhearted people here who will want to do just that."

He sat down beside the children on the bench, and the preacher stood up.

"Let us pray . . ."

After the prayer he announced: "Mr. Carter and I will be here for the rest of the afternoon. Those who wish to interview a child or apply for one will please come forward."

Immediately a big, black-bearded man made his way down the aisle. He was followed by a nicely dressed woman with happy black eyes.

"This is Mr. Thayer, our blacksmith, and this is his wife." The preacher introduced them to Mr. Carter. "He also runs the livery stable."

The boys caught their breath at that. To be taking care of horses was what they all wanted.

"So you folks want a boy?" the preacher said.

Mr. Thayer's laugh rang through the room like a hammer on an anvil. He looked down at his wife and then back toward the bench where he'd been sitting. Following his glance Kevin saw a row of young men, as like to their father as a family of blackbirds.

"Ain't five boys enough? What we want is that black-haired gal." And Mrs. Thayer stepped to the railing and looked straight at Hannah. "Would you like to come to us, my dear? It's all menfolks but me, but you could have your own room."

And so Hannah was the first one chosen. Hiram, George and James were speechless with envy. Except for Dolly's tears, the farewells were cheerful. Her new family bundled her away.

After that some farmers came forward. The preacher vouched for the standing of each one in the community, and the men described their farms, their horses and other livestock. Each boy was to get his schooling, his board and room, and one hundred dollars if he stayed until he was twenty-one. In that way the futures of James, Hiram, and even George were settled. The boys thanked Mr. Carter, promised to write to the society, and went away to their new lives without a backward glance.

"I have one more boy here old enough to do farm work," Mr. Carter told the gathering. But the remaining farmers shook their heads. "That lad!" one said. "There ain't enough of him to hold down a plow." "Look at that white skin," another scoffed. "One day in the sun would sizzle him like a fried tomato."

Elizabeth was picked next.

"My wife wants a girl old enough to help with the children," announced the next man. Mr. Carter suggested Elizabeth. "Kind of small for eight, ain't she?" the man said. "But if that's the oldest one left, she'll have to do. My young'uns is two and three."

"Mr. Phelps is our general storekeeper," the preacher explained. "He and his family live over the store."

Kevin was watching a young couple. The man kept looking toward Dolly or Peter. Then he would confer with his wife again. He seemed to be urging her. She was quietly crying.

The courtroom was clearing out. A bank of snowclouds had come up in the west, people reported. Kevin heard teams brought up outside, and men came stomping in to collect their families. The people who remained, sitting or standing about, were apparently townsfolk, making the most of the entertainment. Who took the children and why would be something to talk about for months.

The sad couple, as Kevin thought of them, came up and asked for Peter. "Their only child died last fall of diphtheria," the preacher said after they left.

Kevin was beginning to wonder if he and Dolly and Maggie would have to sleep at the railroad station again when there was a stir at the door. A snow-powdered figure burst through the crowd and came striding towards the platform. Kevin's heart leaped. Here was a purposeful man, just the kind he, Kevin, would like to work for. The man was small, dark and energetic, his coat was belted closely, his cap had ear flaps, and his legs were encased in leggings.

"I've got orders for two girls," he shouted when he was halfway down the aisle. "I'm a rancher up on Deer Creek. My wife wants one, and Mrs. Higgins wants the other. I'm not too late, am I?" He looked towards the youngsters. "Those two will do fine. Snow's been following me all the way in. If I'm gonna get back, I've got to take 'em and skedaddle."

Mr. Carter looked at the preacher.

"Mr. Jacques," the preacher said quickly.

Mr. Jacques bounded to the railing. "Here's a pair of pretties!" he exclaimed. "My wife and Mrs. Higgins are just a-setting up there on Deer Creek waiting for you."

The little girls looked at him round-eyed.

Everything was quickly arranged. Mr. Carter helped bundle the girls into Mr. Jacques's sleigh, and they dashed away with a jingle of sleighbells.

Kevin shrank back on the bench and wished he could disappear. What would Mr. Carter do with him?

Mr. Carter came back into the room and made his way around the railing. He sat beside Kevin and patted his hand. Kevin caught his lower lip between his teeth. He *would* not cry. He was *not* a criminal, set off from these strangers by a railing.

"I always save my best till last," Mr. Carter said with a smile.

Another stir at the door made them both look up. The man who came in was slim and black-bearded and walked with a limp. Like the other young men, he was bundled into a worn blue army overcoat. An alertness in his manner reminded Kevin of the men who worked on Newspaper Row. He was not surprised when the preacher introduced the newcomer as "the editor of the *Cottonwood Clarion,* our lively newspaper."

The man shook hands with Mr. Carter. "Euclid Smith's my name. I expected to get back to town last night, but my horse threw a shoe. I was over at Grand Island," he explained, "picking up a load of newsprint. The editor there bought more than he could pay for." He glanced at Kevin. "Are they all gone but this one?"

The preacher nodded. "We found fine homes for all the rest," he bragged. "Not one of these children will ever regret coming to our community."

"I'm sure they won't," Mr. Carter agreed.

"I'd like the names of the families who took them," Euclid Smith said, "for next week's paper." The preacher showed him the list.

"Mr. Smith," the preacher said while the editor was copying the list, "weren't you looking for a printer's devil a while back?"

The editor glanced at Kevin. "I need an older lad, one who's had more schooling."

"This boy's eleven and reads very well," Mr.

Carter said quickly. "Come here, Kevin. He's small for his age, that's all. The farmers say he'd burn to a crisp in the fields." Mr. Carter put his arm across Kevin's shoulders.

Euclid Smith straightened from his task of copying and looked Kevin up and down. Kevin stared back, liking what he saw. He hoped suddenly, desperately, that the newspaperman would like *him*.

"I don't have time to look after a child," the editor protested. "Don't even have time to look after myself."

"He won't need looking after," Mr. Carter said. "This boy's bright and quick. It's my guess you can teach him just about anything."

Euclid Smith fingered his beard. Then he asked a surprising question. "Can you cook?"

"Some, sir." Kevin's mother had taught him to peel potatoes and make tea.

"Mr. Smith's a bachelor," the preacher explained.

"What can you read?" Euclid Smith asked.

"Newspapers, sir . . . books."

"How about handwriting? Here—read this." He put the half-copied list into Kevin's hands.

Kevin read aloud: "Hannah Moore, ten, to Mr. and Mrs. Lije Thayer; James Albert, thirteen to

Mr. Harold Connor; Hiram Hostetter, twelve, to Mr. John Swenson—"

"All right, that's enough." He fingered his beard again. "I don't know. Think you'd like printshop work?"

Kevin was nearly speechless with yearning. His 'yes' came out in a whisper from his dry throat.

Euclid Smith looked at the other two men as though he'd been backed into a corner. "I only came to get the story. I'm not sure— I hardly make ends meet as it is."

One of the onlookers lounged up. "Go on, take him, Yuke— What are you waiting for?"

"By George, Jake, I'm waiting for you to pay for your subscription!"

The man called Jake dug in his pocket, produced two quarters, and handed them over. "There you are —four bits." He winked at Kevin.

"All right, by gum, I'll take him," Euclid Smith told Mr. Carter. "I hope you like beans and cornmeal, boy."

Kevin nodded. His throat was too full to speak. He had never thought of such a thing as working in a newspaper office. Mr. Carter was right: the best offer *had* come last.

While Euclid Smith finished copying the list, Kevin said goodbye to Mr. Carter and promised to write.

"Ready to go?" Euclid Smith asked. "We'll stop at the store and get you a tick to sleep on. You're lucky I've got some spare bedding. I suppose you haven't had supper?"

"No, Mr. Smith."

"You don't have to call me Mister," the editor said. "You might as well call me Yuke. Everyone else does, except the preacher. "Well, I usually have popcorn and apples for Sunday supper. That's bachelor fare for you."

Not even the promise of bread and water could have marred Kevin's happiness.

8

The Cottonwood Clarion

On the way to the general store they passed a one-story building with a wooden sign fastened across the front: CLARION OFFICE.

"This is it," Yuke said, giving the wall a pat as he passed. "Solid Nebraska marble."

The wall seemed to be made of squares of brown peat. Then Kevin realized Yuke was joking. Nebraska marble meant sod from the prairie!

The store was open for business at any time because the storekeeper lived upstairs. Yuke bought a mattress tick of tightly woven cotton. Kevin heard footsteps overhead and wondered if some of the steps were Elizabeth's.

Snow began to sift down as they left the store.

"Now," Yuke said, "we'll get some prairie feathers." He led Kevin to a shed behind the Clarion building. "Ho, Jack," he said opening the door, and to Kevin: "Jack's earned his supper tonight. That was a long haul from Grand Island." He tossed hay into Jack's manger and then told Kevin to hold the mattress while he stuffed it. "Prairie feathers" was hay!

Snow was falling thickly when they closed the stable door and went in the back way to the print shop. Kevin followed Yuke through a small room into a big one that smelled of ink.

Yuke lit a lamp. Bulky forms of two presses and three racks of type emerged from the surrounding blackness.

"Brrr!" Yuke rubbed his hands. "I had to let the fire go out while I was gone. Hope the ink didn't freeze. Let's see . . . guess I'll build one in the back, too. I suppose you can build a fire, boy?"

Kevin said, "Yes, sir." He wished Yuke would call him by name.

Kindling and coal were kept in handy bins in one corner of the big room, and Yuke soon had a fire roaring in the shop. He carried the lamp to the back room. It was furnished with a bunk bed, table, chair, stool, some hooks for clothing, a cookstove, and two shelves for dishes. The sod walls had been white-washed and there was a wooden ceiling.

Yuke laid the mattress on the floor. "You'll have to sleep here till I get you a bed." He hauled a rolled-up buffalo hide from under his bunk. "That'll keep the cold out. Make your bed on that." Yuke gave him a quilt and comforter and cotton blankets and set about building a fire in the cookstove. As soon as it was going, he put a hunk of white lard into a skillet and set it to melt. When it was sizzling, he tossed in a handful of corn kernels, clapped a lid on the skillet and rattled it back and forth on the stove lid. Kevin stood warming himself and watching.

"You like popcorn?" Yuke asked.

Kevin smiled and shrugged. "I don't know."

"What? You never had popcorn? How long you been in this country?"

Kevin counted. "Going on four months."

"That explains it. Over supper you must tell me about yourself." He had to raise his voice to speak above the racket in the skillet. Kevin guessed why it was called *pop* corn, and he understood even better when Yuke removed the lid. The little golden kernels had exploded into solid white snowflakes. Yuke set the black iron frying pan on the table, sprinkled salt over the contents and disappeared into the shop. He returned with four golden apples.

"The apple barrel, potatoes, onions—I keep them all in the shop so they won't freeze."

They sat at the table in their coats, eating popcorn and apples and drinking hot coffee.

Kevin told Yuke how he and his mother had started for America and his mother had died aboard ship. He told Yuke about Uncle Michael's being in jail and how he had become a newsboy and slept on the street until he found out about the Newsboys' Lodging House.

"You *can* take care of yourself," Yuke admitted. He questioned Kevin about the New York dailies— how many pages they ran and how often they managed to print extras.

The fire in the cookstove was allowed to go out, and the room grew cold. Yuke stood up and stretched. He measured two dippers of water into an iron kettle and poured in a cupful of grain. Saying, "We'll have boiled wheat for breakfast," he took the kettle into the shop, set it on the stove there, and banked that fire. It was early, but Yuke, too, had had a tiring day, hauling his newsprint. They peeled down to their underwear and climbed into their beds.

The fresh hay felt as soft as the lodging house beds. Kevin said to himself that a prayer of thanksgiving was called for. Here he was, in a more exciting place than he ever could have thought of.

He was almost asleep when the most forlorn howl he had ever heard brought him sitting up and wide awake. The howl changed to a series of yips. Was it the banshee? He felt the hair rise on his head.

"Yuke!" he whispered urgently.

"Eh? What?" Yuke, too, had been nearly asleep. It was a relief just to hear his voice.

"What's that noise?"

"Oh— Coyotes. Nothing to be afraid of."

"They sound horrible!"

"No— They're just singing to each other. They'll quiet down pretty soon. Go to sleep."

IT WAS STILL DARK when he woke next morning to the smell of boiling coffee. Yuke had been up some time. He had built up the fires and shoveled snow from the path to the outhouse and the shed. Kevin scrambled into his clothes, and Yuke sent him to shovel snow off the wooden walk in front of the building. When he finished, Yuke filled two bowls with steaming mounds of boiled wheat, over which they poured molasses and milk.

Yuke said, "It's Monday, so you'd better start school. I'm boiling some water. That's the dishpan, and that's the washpan. Wash the dishes, and also yourself. When you're through, come out and I'll show you the type cases."

Kevin hurried through both chores. In the shop he found Yuke standing before one of the type racks. He was holding a little metal half-box in his left hand and dropping into it bits of metal picked from the type case, seemingly at random. However, he indicated a printed piece of paper propped in front of him.

"I'm setting this story in type. This thing in my hand is a composing stick. When it's full of lines of type, I'll slide them onto that wooden tray there. That's called a galley. See those other trays full of type?"

"Yes, sir."

"We're through with those. You realize that after the paper's printed, all the type has to be thrown back into the cases—each letter into its proper box?"

Kevin nodded.

"That's one place a printer's devil helps out. And Heaven help you if you put the letters back wrong. First you'll have to learn the case. There are two cases, actually—" He made Kevin sit up on a high stool while he explained. "This upper case propped at the back contains capital letters. This lower case in front contains the small letters and punctuation. See, here's a comma, here are the e's, the a's." He picked up one of the tiny pieces of lead, showing Kevin the "e" on one end of it. Then he brought over one of the old galleys. From it he picked up a chunk of type, which kept its shape of lines and words because he knew how to hold it. He proceeded to take it apart, letter by letter, throwing each piece unhesitatingly into the square where it belonged.

Kevin watched, mesmerized by the quick dance of Yuke's long fingers.

"There—" Yuke tossed the last letter and stacked the lead pieces that lay between each line. "Think you can learn to do that?"

"I'll try," Kevin said willingly.

Yuke seized a piece of paper and drew a quick outline of a type case with all the squares. He marked a letter in each one. "Here— Study this when you have time." He took Kevin to the door and pointed across the snowy waste to an unpainted building. Kevin saw small figures making their way towards it.

Yuke dug in his pocket and produced a coin. "Stop by the store. You'll need a slate and a slate pencil, I suppose. The editor before me left one or two schoolbooks. I'll try to dig them out." He swung a hand toward an overloaded desk.

The clear morning light showed a grand collection on and around it. Kevin noted a bundle of newspapers, most of them rolled into wrappers, a horse collar, a rifle and a stack of posters advertising land for sale. The space beneath the desk was filled with a wooden box that said NAILS and two bags of oats.

Kevin stepped eagerly into the wintry day.

"See you at noon," Yuke said.

It felt strange to be setting off for school, having done nothing more than wash the dishes and fill the coal scuttles.

He bought his slate and arrived at the building just as the teacher called everyone in. Hannah looked glad to see Kevin; dear little Elizabeth stuck out her tongue. They had no time to talk. The teacher had them sit in the back while he read a chapter from the Bible. Then he called them up front and had them read aloud so he could decide what grades they belonged in.

Red-faced, Hannah and Elizabeth admitted they could not read it all. The prairie children tittered. The teacher seemed surprised when Kevin read the passage indicated. The schoolroom tittered again at his brogue.

Kevin was sent to sit with the big boys. Hannah and Elizabeth had to sit up front with the little children.

Tad Williams, the boy next to Kevin, shared his book. It was an American history, a subject totally new to Kevin. He studied happily. The teacher worked hard with Hannah and Elizabeth so they could catch up with the first graders.

As soon as recess was declared, the three New York children rushed together to compare notes.

"Who took you?" they demanded of Kevin.

He told them how the newspaper editor had been talked into taking him.

Hannah said she had been given a beautiful bedroom with a crocheted bedspread and white curtains made of flour sacks. "Of course the room's cold now," she said, "but when spring comes, I'm going to spend all my spare time in it."

"Are they working you hard?" Kevin asked.

Hannah shook her head. "Mrs. Thayer says she had so many boys, she just *had* to teach them to help in the kitchen."

"And you, Elizabeth?"

"My job is to look after Mrs. Phelps's babies so she can work faster. Last night we had meat and corn pudding and apple pie—all we could eat."

"We had popcorn and apples," Kevin said. "That's 'cause Yuke is a bachelor. He calls his cooking 'batching it.' "

They talked about their new homes until the bell called them back inside.

At noon Kevin and Elizabeth crossed the snowy field to Main Street. As soon as Kevin entered the print shop, Yuke pointed to the water bucket. "Fill that, Kevin, me lad. The well's over on the courthouse square. Be quick. The potatoes are nearly done." When Kevin returned, Yuke sent him to fill the big teakettle from the rainwater barrel out back so there would be hot water for dishwashing.

Another man was working in the shop. He

joined them at the dinner table. "Dandy Miles," Yuke told Kevin. "He's my printer. Lives at the hotel. He puts up with my cooking at noon."

"That's because I get a good meal at night," Dandy said with a wink at Kevin. He was older than Yuke. Despite the ink under his fingernails, he did look like a dandy. He was closely shaven and wore a white, boiled shirt and black sleeveguards to keep his cuffs clean.

They dined on boiled potatoes and fried salt pork. Yuke said he would set a batch of bread to rise that evening and bake it in the morning.

Kevin washed the dinner dishes, and then it was time to go back to school, but he lingered to watch Dandy. With the composing stick in his left hand, Dandy's right hand moved over the case like lightning, dropping each piece of type into its place in line, holding it there with his left thumb while he reached for the next. He never glanced at the type itself, so sure was he that he had taken the right letter from the right box. Kevin could see why the letters had to be put back exactly.

Yuke said, "When school's out this afternoon, you can start throwing type in. That way, you'll learn fast."

Kevin tore himself away and ran back to school. Sharing Tad's other books, he thought how each printed page had been set, letter by letter, from cases like those at the *Clarion*. Perhaps some day he, too, would be a printer. Or even an editor, like Yuke.

9

Printer's Devil

How the first week flew! Everything was exciting. Mornings Kevin could hardly wait to get to the school yard and afternoons he could hardly wait to get back to the *Clarion*.

Any news in town quickly found its way to the newspaper office. Much of it came from Phelps's store next door, which was a gathering place for idlers. The men who had staked claims and built shanties now had nothing to do but wait for spring. They rode into town to buy food and tobacco and ease their loneliness. If the sun shone, they stood outside watching the teamsters come and go, hauling lumber, coal and food over frozen trails to outlying settlements.

Kevin saw Hannah and Elizabeth only at school. Afterwards they all had to hurry home to do chores.

Hannah had easy work—sewing and mending and helping cook. Mrs. Thayer said Hannah was too young to do heavy work. It would make her round-shouldered and old before her time. Mrs. Thayer hired the big girl from the hotel for the mopping and washing.

The Thayer boys were charmed with their new sister. One of the first things they did was give her a pony. Kevin and Elizabeth, crossing Main Street with buckets of water, watched Hannah and her brothers going off for a gallop on the prairie. Elizabeth stuck out her tongue, but Kevin was glad for Hannah, and only a little jealous. He remembered how the boys on the train had scoffed when Hannah said she was going to have a horse.

Elizabeth didn't have to work hard, either. She was rapidly learning to read, and had almost stopped swearing.

Kevin admired Yuke with his whole heart. One of the reasons he hurried in from school was to see what exciting thing Yuke was doing. Yuke talked while he worked. He even talked while he set type. Of course, he often put in the wrong letters, unlike Dandy, who could set a whole galley without error.

"It must be Kevin's fault," Yuke would say. "That boy hasn't learned to throw my case *yet*."

Dandy put his own type away, but the fact was that Kevin *had* learned the case, and was careful to put the letters back right.

"You made as many mistakes before he came," Dandy would reply.

Kevin rather liked Yuke's mistakes because Yuke let him make the corrections. They were easy to fix. Yuke taught him how to roll ink on the galleys and take a proof of the column of type and read it for errors. The lines of type were like a mirror reflection of the impression on paper. The letters and words ran backwards, so that it was easier to look at the type upside down. Then the words ran the right direction, and one could read the letters upside down. Kevin would find the letter that was wrong, coax the type out with a flat piece of metal called a composing rule, and drop in the correct letter.

Sometimes Yuke sang. He had a good voice, and he knew songs with endless verses.

"Listen to this!" he said one evening.

Kevin was at his usual job of distributing used type into the case. He was also keeping an eye on the kitchen stove where Yuke's cornbread was baking. Dandy had left for the day.

Yuke sat beside the heating stove, going through exchanges—the papers from other prairie towns for which Yuke exchanged copies of the *Clarion*. Editors all sent each other copies and in this way kept in touch with what was happening all across the plains. Yuke read exchanges whenever he could spare a few minutes and looked for items to fill out the sparsity of Cottonwood City news.

"Listen! This is from—" He paused to look at the paper's masthead. "The *Call*, Pearlette, Kansas, written by the editor:

> *I am looking rather seedy now while hold-*
> *ing down my claim,*
> *And my victuals are not always of the best;*
> *And the mice play shyly round me as I*
> *nestle down to rest*
> *In my little old sod shanty in the West*
> *Yet I rather like the novelty of living in this*
> *way,*

*Though my bill of fare is always rather
    tame,
But I'm happy as a clam on the land of
    Uncle Sam,
In my little old sod shanty on my claim.*

"You can sing it to the tune of 'Little Old Log Cabin in the Lane,' it says. Here's the chorus:

*The hinges are of leather and the windows
    have no glass
While the board roof lets the howling
    blizzard in,
And I hear the hungry kiyote as he creeps
    up through the grass
Round my little old sod shanty on my claim.*

*Oh, when I left my eastern home, a bachelor
    so gay,
To try to win my way to wealth and fame,
I little thought that I'd come down to
    burning twisted hay
In my little old sod shanty on the claim.*

"That will fill up space," Yuke said with satisfaction.

Suddenly Kevin sniffed something burning. He made a dash for the kitchen stove. Sure enough, the cornbread had burned on the bottom.

That evening Kevin learned a new job—kicking the pedal of the job press. With each kick it printed a sheet of paper. This was work that could be done after supper. The lamp Yuke used at the type case threw enough light for Kevin to feed the sheets of paper.

Yuke began setting the poem in type, singing it as he worked.

Kevin could hardly remember when he had been so happy. He was full of baked beans and cornbread, and was helping Yuke to run the printshop.

"Why is he burning twisted hay?" Kevin asked, as Yuke came to that verse again.

"He didn't have anything else," Yuke answered. "There's no wood on the prairie. Once the buffalo chips and cow chips are used up, there's nothing but wild grass. You have to twist it tight to make it burn any time at all. Phelps has a newfangled cookstove for sale that does the twisting for you. It's called a hay-burner."

Kevin looked appreciatively at the coal bin in the corner. It was more than half full.

Late in the week, the weather turned warm. The sun shone brightly, there was no wind, and the snow disappeared, leaving the prairie brown and bare. Even though it was not yet February, men were arriving in town to take up land. They came on horseback, driving wagons, and by train. If they came by train, they hired buggies at the livery stable and drove out to look the country over. Some bought from the railroad company, but most were looking for free land. When they found an unclaimed quarter-section they liked, they had to hurry back to the land office in Grand Island to register it. Cottonwood City, which had seemed so quiet, now seemed to bustle with activity.

"We have lots of coal left over," Kevin said. "Winter isn't bad out here."

"Hah!" Yuke said. "You don't think it's over, do you?"

"Isn't it?"

"Not by a long shot. All those greenhorns wandering out of here looking for land . . . they'll get caught up in a blizzard one of these days."

"What will happen to them?"

"They could freeze to death. Snow swirls so thick you can't see, and the wind seems to come from every direction. Men who've been at the barn feeding stock have walked right past their houses and out onto the prairie. The first editor that was here got caught in a blizzard, coming back from Grand Island. Scared him so he went back East."

Kevin eyed Yuke.

Yuke said, "No, I'm not telling tales to scare you, boy."

"Couldn't I follow the road?"

"How can you see the road when it's covered with blowing snow? No, sir!"

But when the sky was so blue and the sun so bright and warm, Kevin found it hard to believe in such storms.

"I have a claim myself," Yuke said. "Guess I'd better ride out there on Sunday and make sure nobody's jumped it."

"What's 'jumped it'?"

"Moved in. There's a sod house on it.

"I thought you had to live there," Kevin said.

"Six months a year. We'll move there come spring, and ride Jack back and forth."

"What will I ride?"

"You can ride behind me. Jack won't notice such a featherweight."

Kevin couldn't wait to begin, even if he had to ride behind Yuke. He wondered every time he watered and fed Jack how it would feel to sit on his back.

"Where is your claim?"

"South about three miles."

"May I go with you to look at it?"

"If the weather holds."

Yuke finished setting the poem and dropped the half-column of type into the page form. He made it take up more space by dropping in thin strips of lead between the lines. Then he took the quoin key and began tightening the quoins. They were metal wedges that moved against each other to make everything else tight. All the type for the page had to fit so snugly together inside the metal frame that nothing would slip and fall out when the page was moved from the marble slab where Yuke put it together to the flatbed of the press.

If the man making up the page got careless and didn't get everything tight, a line or several lines of type might drop out onto the floor. Then the mixed-up type was said to be pied, and the air was blue with curses. Sorting pied type was much harder than simply putting used type back into the case. Sometimes even different sizes got mixed together when a chunk fell out. Yuke had already introduced Kevin to a dusty box where a lot of pied type had been dumped and conveniently forgotten, awaiting the arrival of someone like Kevin.

Tomorrow was Friday, the day the paper went to press. Kevin suggested he could stay home from school and help print it, but Yuke shook his head. "When you get home, you can fold," he said.

Half the paper was already printed. The *Cottonwood Clarion* was one sheet, folded, making four pages. The inside pages had been printed in Chicago. That was the paper, called ready-print, that Yuke had hauled from Grand Island. The two pages were filled with essays and recipes and jokes and advertisements for hair tonic and farm machinery and patent medicine.

The Washington press stood waiting to print the other half.

At noon next day Kevin came home to find both men ink-smeared and ill-tempered. A part of the press had broken, and the blacksmith had taken his time about fixing it.

Kevin built up the fire in the cookstove and boiled potatoes and fried salt pork. The men swallowed their food and turned back to the job at hand. When Kevin got home after school, the repair had been made; the papers were coming off the press. Yuke showed Kevin how to put the edges together and give a swift stroke with a ruler to make a sharp fold. Each paper had to be folded twice. Yuke's pencil flew, writing addresses on brown wrappers for mailing. He cooked a pot of paste out of flour and water and handed Kevin a paint brush. Kevin brushed paste on the wrappers and rolled the papers in them. After that he carried them in a great washbucket to the post office at the back of the drug store. He made two trips before the post office closed. The rest would be mailed in the morning.

Many were going to subscribers back East. When Kevin asked why, Yuke said, "Those Easterners are thinking of moving out here. That's why our masthead says: "Calling the attention of the emigrant to the Upper Cottonwood Valley as a desirable field of settlement and investment."

A stack of *Clarions* was put on Yuke's desk in the front office to sell to newcomers and farmers who would be in town on Saturday.

Because of the breakdown, it was nearly ten o'clock before the last sheet was run.

"Another week's issue," Yuke said with a yawn.

Dandy went off to the nearest saloon. Yuke and Kevin tumbled into bed.

Saturday morning Kevin was scarcely dressed before he heard people up front, coming to buy the paper and staying to discuss politics and weather.

"Our trip may be off tomorrow," Yuke said, returning to the kitchen. "The oldtimers say a storm's coming."

Kevin glanced out the window. A week ago the glass had been covered with frost. Now one could see through it to the blue sky. It was the bright, crisp kind of day that made you want to get out and frisk, even though the thawing ground was muddy.

Saturday, however, was still a working day, although with an air of relaxation. The paper was out for another week. Dandy arrived late, looking haggard, and drank several cups of coffee before he would talk to anyone.

Kevin's chores were not changed. He still had to wash dishes and sweep the shop and carry water, but he didn't have to hurry doing it. He met Tad Williams at the pump, and Tad showed him the wooden chain he was whittling and promised to show him how to make one.

Yuke fried stacks of pancakes for dinner, and they ate them with molasses and melted butter.

That afternoon a farmer came in to pay for a subscription. Yuke came into the back room with a grin. He held up a big jackrabbit. "Rabbit stew for Sunday dinner," he announced. "This is just part of the price. He promised two more rabbits later on." He took it out back to skin.

For supper Kevin and Yuke had baked beans and cornbread again. While they ate, a bucket of water from the rain barrel steamed on the stove, heating for the Saturday night bath. Kevin had never taken a whole bath. Except for the showers at the lodging house, the folks he knew washed themselves a little at a time, but Yuke said that out here there was room for Kevin to undress completely and sit himself in the washbucket. Yuke put the bucket, which was like a small tub with a handle, on one side of the cookstove. Kevin undressed and sat in it with his feet out and washed himself. Yuke sat on the other side of the stove and read the exchanges aloud.

Kevin washed fast. Getting wet all at once seemed crazy. The side of him next to the stove was warm enough—too warm—but the other side was freezing. By the time he stood up to dry himself on the rough linen towel, his teeth were chattering.

"I had Mrs. Phelps make you a union suit so's you'd have a change." Yuke lowered the paper and tossed Kevin a folded garment of red flannel. "Hop into that and get into bed."

Kevin put it on. It was one piece, like men wore instead of pants buttoning onto a top. It was a little long. Mrs. Phelps had left room for him to grow.

Yuke added hot water to the water in the wash-bucket, turned down the lamp in case anyone walked by the uncurtained back window, and took his bath.

Kevin began to feel warm and tingling. He breathed deep of the smell of new cloth. Yuke seemed offhand and careless, but underneath he was thoughtful and kind. He was singing now, the new song.

> *My clothes are plastered o'er with dough,*
> *I'm looking like a fright,*
> *And everything is scattered round the*
> *room ...*

Kevin fell asleep on the chorus.

10

The Shanty on the Claim

Sunday morning the sun was slanting across flattened weeds when Kevin crossed the street to the well. When he returned, Yuke was squinting at the northwest sky. He said, "If the weather is still nice after church, we'll take a chance. Jack needs exercise."

On the cookstove the rabbit was stewing with potatoes and turnips. They ate mush for breakfast and dressed for church. Yuke put on his best coat. He scraped soot from inside the stove lid and blacked his boots. Kevin did likewise.

When Kevin stepped inside the church building, he remembered how frightened he had been one week ago. Now he noticed how new the church looked. Walls, benches and the pulpit were still the creamy color of new wood. The room smelled warmly of people and damp wool.

Sunday school class for children was up front on one side. The class for those who considered themselves 'young people' was on the other side. The married people met at the back.

Hannah arrived with the Thayers. She came and sat by Kevin. Under her coat she had on a new dress, gray, with tiny pink roses. Her cheeks were pink from the cold air, and her eyes sparkled.

Elizabeth came with Mr. Phelps, who was the Sunday school superintendent and led the singing. Mrs. Thayer played the organ.

"That's *our* organ," Hannah whispered. "It's only loaned to the church. When we get it back, Mama's going to teach me to play it."

"Mama!" Kevin exclaimed.

Hannah looked self-conscious. "That's what she told me to call her. And Mr. Thayer 'papa', and I'm to think of the boys as my brothers."

That was nice for Hannah, Kevin thought, but he was glad he could call Yuke by name. He had had a real mother and father.

There were three young ladies in the young people's class. Kevin watched the Thayer boys and Yuke talking with them.

After Sunday school Elizabeth went home to stay with the Phelps children so Mrs. Phelps could attend church. For church each family sat together. Kevin hoped everyone would notice that he was sitting beside Yuke. The bare room rang with the singing. Yuke's voice, strong and sure, seemed to encourage the rest of the congregation.

As soon as church was over and Kevin stepped outside, he looked at the northwest sky. Such weather-watching was becoming a habit. The sky still looked blue.

"Are we going?" he asked Yuke.

"Sure thing!" Yuke said. "We won't even wash the dishes."

They ate the rabbit stew quickly, good as it was, with the last of the bread. Leaving the dishes on the table, they went to the stable and saddled Jack. Yuke led him outside.

"Hold him a minute." He handed the reins to Kevin. Kevin held the well-oiled leather strips in one hand and patted Jack's nose with the other.

Yuke disappeared through the door and came

out carrying a rifle. "Who knows, we might see some game," he remarked, but Kevin remembered the claim jumpers. That was the object of Yuke's trip, to check on the claim.

Yuke swung into the saddle, and Jack began to prance. "Whoa, boy!" he said. He reached down to Kevin. "Here, take my hand. Put your foot on mine and swing up behind me."

But Kevin's legs weren't long enough. He couldn't get his foot up to the stirrup.

Yuke laughed. That was another good thing about him: he was never impatient when Kevin couldn't do things. "Over here, then," he said, and coaxed Jack to the chopping block.

Kevin jumped up on the block. From there it was easy to put one foot on Yuke's boot toe and swing himself up behind Yuke onto Jack's shiny brown rump.

"Hang on!" Yuke said and clucked to the horse.

Sitting back there wasn't as comfortable as Kevin had expected, especially when Jack began dancing down the street. Kevin's teeth rattled. He hung on, jouncing up and down. They trotted around the corner and down the road to the railroad tracks.

"You all right?" Yuke asked over his shoulder.

"I'll have to let him run a bit to the get the kinks out. Brace your feet on the backs of my legs."

Kevin did as Yuke suggested. When the awful trotting began again, his feet, at least, did not flop around. He clung to the saddle's croup with both hands. Suddenly the ride smoothed out. Jack was cantering. Hummocks of brown grass flew past, a long way below, but soft to fall on, if worst came to worst.

After a short while Yuke pulled the horse to a walk, and then the ride became very pleasant, and Kevin could look around, although there wasn't much to see. The line where land met sky might have been drawn with a rule, but the land itself was made up of long swells, with low places between, like frozen waves. Some of the low spots had dry creek beds. In the deeper ones snowbanks lingered.

They watched for rabbits, but nothing moved over the whole expanse. High in the blue Yuke spotted a hawk, but they saw no other living thing. Even the two claim shanties they passed were deserted.

"That's good," Yuke said. "Those shanties belong to folks in town. The womenfolk will move out here, come spring. The law says a man's family has to live on his claim six months of the year. So the wives and children live on the claims while the men go on running their businesses. Ain't much for a man to do on a claim, once he's planted the ten acres the law demands. When the five years are up, and a man owns the land, he can borrow money from a bank for machinery. You can't do much farming out here without machinery.

"Here we are," he announced, passing two stakes in the ground. "Here's my bet with Uncle Sam."

"Your bet?"

Yuke laughed. "A homesteader has to pay fourteen dollars to file a claim. You know that?"

"Yes."

"Well, folks say Uncle Sam is betting eighty acres to fourteen dollars that they'll starve to death before their five years are up so the government won't have to give them the land. I'm one of the lucky ones, having the *Clarion*."

Yuke rode down into a dry wash and there, built against the bank, was his sod house. It looked like more of the dirt bank, except that it had a weathered wooden door and a board-covered window.

They dismounted, Kevin sliding down first, glad to be able to straighten his legs. Yuke tied Jack to the hitching rail and opened the door. Kevin peeked over his shoulder.

Light was coming through a big hole in the roof. On the floor beneath was a big pile of dirt. The corners were full of unmelted snow.

"I was afraid of that," Yuke said. "The snow last month made the sod too heavy and broke the boards. That's soon fixed."

Peering around Yuke's elbow, Kevin saw a table, a chair, a bench and an iron bedstead.

"I have the window sash in the shop," Yuke was saying. "The shutter comes off, and the sash goes in."

Kevin turned away. The abandoned shanty was so desolate and cold that the outdoors looked cheery by comparison. Then he saw, edging over the rise, a steely-gray cloud.

"Look." He pointed.

"Whee-oo!" Yuke whistled. "Let's head for home!"

He untied Jack and mounted. Kevin skinned up onto the hitching rail and clambered onto Jack's back from there. They set out at a steady pace over the flat brown prairie.

Speedily the cloud covered the sky, contemptuously blotting out the westering sun.

Yuke clucked, and Jack began to trot. The jouncing gave Kevin a pain in his side, but he was glad to be going faster.

When the wind hit, its icy blast cut straight through his layers of clothing, finding its way to every square inch of his skin. If he tried to see where they were going, it made his eyes water.

"There we are!" Yuke's voice blew back. As they topped a rise, he pulled Jack to a walk. Kevin peered around Yuke's arm. Sure enough, straight ahead lay the scattered buildings of Cottonwood City, like a toy town huddling away from the great black cloud.

"We'll make it," Yuke shouted. "But you see how fast these things come up."

They were stabling Jack when the blizzard hit. The crash of wind shook the shed roof, sending dribbles of dirt through the cracks between the boards. Yuke rubbed Jack down, and Kevin brought water from the barrel. By the time they finished, the snow was blowing so wildly they had to grope their way to the back door. The snow wasn't falling. It seemed to be blowing straight across the face of the earth. If the wind blew the snow so hard it couldn't fall, would it keep right on going, down across Nebraska and Kansas, into Indian Territory? Would it ever fall before it got so far south it turned to rain?

They flung themselves inside and slammed the door.

"Whooo!" Yuke shivered. He shook snow from his hat and muffler. "Let's hope nobody's caught in it." He rubbed his hands and began to build up the fire.

A picture of Yuke's shanty came to Kevin's mind. He could see it with snow swirling into the dark, sour-smelling room. By comparison, the *Clarion*'s back room, with its unmade beds and mud-tracked floor, was homey. Without being told, Kevin smoothed the covers and went into the printshop to get the broom. When he came back, Yuke was melting lard. Kevin next heard the sound of corn poured into the pan. He finished sweeping, put away the broom, and fetched his speller and arithmetic from where he'd dropped them Friday afternoon.

Outside, the wind howled round the building and rattled the stovepipe, but it had no effect on the thick sod walls. Frost began to creep back up the windowpanes, and the floor grew cold. However, the lamp's yellow glow, the smell of popcorn and kerosene and apples made the room seem cozy. Kevin studied while they ate. Yuke was writing a letter. If they were still hungry after the popcorn, a good half of last night's Indian pudding stood on the back of the stove.

Yuke signed his letter with a flourish and looked up. "There! That's to the girl I'm engaged to. She's coming out in the spring."

Kevin's heart thudded. Oh, no! "You mean you'll get married?"

"I hope so!"

"You won't want *me* then," Kevin said gruffly. Married women had babies. They wouldn't want half-grown boys around.

"Sure we will," Yuke answered cheerfully. "I wrote her about you."

"There won't be room for me," Kevin said, almost with satisfaction, picturing again the forlorn inside of the sod house. He wouldn't be sorry not to live there. It was worse than the meanest hut in Ireland.

"We'll make room," Yuke promised. "We'll hang a curtain between the beds."

Inwardly Kevin sighed. He should have known things couldn't be as good as they seemed.

11

Cold, Wintry Weather

All night and all next day the blizzard raged; the wind howled, and blowing snow filled the air. There was no question of school. Kevin didn't even have to go to the well. Whenever Yuke or he went outside for chores, they brought back a bucket of snow and melted that.

Dandy came to work, guided by the board walk. He reported that two home-seekers from Illinois had returned to town safely because they had had sense enough to let their horses from the livery stable find their way home.

Kevin had plenty to do around the shop. He kept the fire going strong. The stove grew red hot, but bitter cold still invaded the room. Where the job press stood by a window, it was so cold that the ink froze. Yuke had to put off printing handbills until the weather changed.

Throwing used type back into the case, Kevin's fingers grew numb. The howl of the wind outside drowned the busy click of the types as Dandy slung them into his stick. Kevin was glad when Yuke began to sing:

> *Oh, jolly is the miller boy who lives by the*
> > *mill;*
> > *The mill goes around with a right good*
> > *will*
> *One hand in the hopper and the other in*
> > *the sack*
> > *The ladies go forward and the gents turn*
> > *back.*
>
> *Oh, it snows and it blows and it's cold*
> > *wintry weather*
> > *In comes the farmer, a-selling of his cider*
> *You be the reaper and I'll be the binder*
> > *Lost my true love, and where shall I find*
> > *her?*

Dandy was sporting a pair of fingerless gloves he called mitts. One of the ladies at the saloon had knitted them for him. They left his fingers free to pick up the type, but of course it was his fingers that the cold attacked. From time to time he had to stop and warm them at the lamp chimney.

Yuke said, "I wrote Sally I needed mitts like those. If she doesn't knit them soon, winter will be over."

"Go see Annie at the saloon," Dandy said with a laugh. "She'll make you a pair. She asks about you."

"No, thanks," Yuke said shortly.

Kevin decided Sally must be Yuke's sweetheart. "Where does she live?" he asked.

"Euclid, Michigan," Yuke replied.

"Euclid, eh?" Dandy raised his eyes from the case. "Were you named for the town, or was the town named for you?"

"It was named for my grandfather," Yuke said.

"So you're pretty big pumpkins back there?"

"Not me. My older brothers took over the newspaper business when Pa died. After the War, I figured I'd better strike out on my own. They would have made room for me. Sally wanted to settle there, but

I decided to heed Greeley's advice and go West."

" 'Go West, young man, and grow up with the country,' " Dandy quoted.

"That's right. I was a journeyman printer in Nebraska City when Reverend Scott and the rest of the Cottonwood City promoters came there. They were looking for an editor. They offered me the works here on easy payments. I could take over the last editor's claim into the bargain, so here I am."

Kevin waited for Dandy to tell what had brought him to Cottonwood City, but he didn't. He and Yuke began discussing matters of their craft: the secret of glue making, and how to mold rollers and cast the lead slugs that filled in around the type to leave white space.

Dandy often told funny stories about other places he had worked, but he never explained why he moved around so much. When Kevin asked Yuke, he said, "He's a tramping printer, that's all. They can't stay put. They like to keep going. They're looking for the perfect shop. Maybe someday they'll find it."

That blizzard-filled afternoon Yuke handed Kevin his compositor's stick and let him set his first paragraph of type. Letter by letter Kevin set it in the stick and then pulled a proof on a scrap of paper. There was the item:

> The emqty store buildings in Cottonwood City are fast disaqqearing, showing that this city is on a steady increase. Several brick structures will be built as sqring oqens.

Yuke looked over Kevin's shoulder and laughed. "You forgot to watch your p's and q's!"

Kevin made the corrections. His next item came out perfect. It said:

> Miss Harriet Braun is now keeping books for her father at the German Lumberyard, taking the place of William Ives. Miss Harriet is a bright girl and can be of great assistance to her father.

After that he set a few more lines, and then he was glad to get up and fill the coal scuttle and warm his hands.

Monday was Yuke's bread baking day. The dark,

howling afternoon was drawing to a close when he brought the loaves from the oven. Dandy put on his coat and muffler and felt his way to Phelps's store next door. He returned with a paper-wrapped mound of butter. They gathered round the shop stove and had tea and fresh bread and butter.

Kevin thought maybe he would learn to do more of the cooking. He could ask Yuke to teach him to make bread, and maybe Hannah would tell him how to make biscuits and piecrust. Then Yuke wouldn't need to get married.

The middle of the second day, the storm let up. The day after that Kevin went back to school. The prairie was one vast stretch of white. Despite the wind, the snow had piled up on the ground and drifted around everything that got in its way. The air was bitterly cold, and clouds still hovered.

"Keep an eye on the northwest," Yuke said when Kevin set out. "It feels like there's more coming. If Mr. Olson decides to close school, don't fool around. Come straight home, understand?"

At school the Thayer boys and Joe, the saloon-keeper's son, considered themselves the most weather-wise.

"Bet you we get sent home early," Charlie

Thayer said at noon.

Sure enough, before afternoon recess, wind struck the building like a blow, making everyone jump. Tom, the older of the two Thayer boys in school, interrupted the class that was reciting. He asked permission to go out and look at the sky.

Mr. Olson refused. "In fifteen minutes you can do all the looking you wish." He went on with the spelling lesson.

The pupils not reciting eyed one another uneasily. Wind rattled the building and snowflakes began swirling past the window, but no one dared say more. Mr. Olson was a strict disciplinarian, enforcing his discipline with a strap.

Tad Williams wrote on his slate and pushed it in front of Kevin. *He is new out here*, Kevin read.

As soon as Mr. Olson announced recess, the Thayer boys rushed out the door. They were back in a second. Charlie hurried Hannah into her coat and hood. Seventeen-year-old Tom Thayer marched up to Mr. Olson.

"It's a blizzard, sure enough, and it's bad already," he reported.

"Very well," Mr. Olson said. "School dismissed. The School Board has given permission to dismiss school early when a blizzard threatens."

"It's not threatening," Tad Williams muttered, pulling on rabbit-skin mittens. "It's here."

Everyone but Mr. Olson crowded into the cloakroom. The Thayers were ready first. Tom Thayer started to open the outside door again, but it was torn from his hands and blown back against the wall. The full force of wind and snow hurled in upon the pupils. Girls squealed, boys shouted.

With Tom leading and all of them holding hands, the Thayers and the teamster's children fought their way into the blinding, shrieking whiteness. The teamster's house lay beyond the Thayers'. It was possible to miss a house in such a blinding storm, but the Thayer boys seemed to know what they were doing. As soon as they stepped through the door, they were lost from sight. Mr. Olson had to add his strength before the remaining boys could close the door.

He was now taking the blizzard seriously. "I'd never have believed it," he said, almost apologetically. "I was—er—resting last Sunday when the other one began. I had no idea it happened so quickly."

Joe, the saloonkeeper's son, organized the remaining pupils to walk towards Main Street. Once they reached the board walk, the various ones could be dropped off at their homes or their fathers' stores. The stationmaster's son would have to go two blocks further south, but the teacher was boarding there and would be with him. They would be bound to strike the railroad tracks.

They set out in a line, holding hands, with the younger children spaced between older ones who could be counted on not to let go of them. Mr. Olson brought up the rear.

How cold it was! Far colder than at noon, when they had all played in the snow. The first gust blew Kevin's muffler away from his face. He had not wrapped it tightly enough. Driven snow stung his cheeks. His nose would probably freeze, but he dare not let go either of the first grader's hand or Elizabeth's in order to rewrap the muffler.

It was like trying to walk through endless, icy featherbeds. Impossible to tell how far they had gone, or where they were going. He could barely make out Elizabeth's head and shoulders. The person beyond her was invisible. Too late he thought of counting steps. Anyway, how many steps was it to Main Street? Perhaps Joe knew. He stumbled along, his arms outstretched, the bitter wind cutting to his armpits. He wondered what good it had done to learn to take care of himself in New York City. That knowledge was no good at all out here.

He knew how easy it was to get lost in a thick Irish fog, but in a fog one didn't freeze to death. Here the wind seemed to howl down from the North Pole. Finding people on the prairie, it was determined to destroy them.

About the time Kevin began to fear they were lost, he felt Elizabeth's arm move sharply upward. The next instant he kicked the boardwalk. Joe's path had brought them straight to Phelps's General Store, and they all filed in. Everyone was accounted for. Elizabeth stayed and the doctor's children from across the street. The teacher and the stationmaster's boy went south toward the station. The rest proceeded along Main Street.

Kevin bounced thankfully through the door of the *Clarion* Office, stomping his feet to restore the circulation. He was surprised to see Yuke in army overcoat and muffler, pulling on mittens.

"Where in tarnation have you been?" Yuke shouted. Dandy appeared behind him, type stick in hand.

"Mr. Olson wouldn't let us go!" Kevin declared.

"He made Tom Thayer wait till recess to look at the weather."

"What!" Yuke exclaimed. "Come back to the stove and tell me what happened. I'll make some tea."

Kevin explained while Yuke checked his nose and ears to make sure they weren't frozen. He made him take off his shoes and stockings and wiggle his toes. The blood flowing back into his extremities made him gasp and cry out at the pain, but Yuke said he should be glad; that meant nothing was frostbitten.

Yuke ground his teeth over the teacher's stupidity and sat down to write an angry editorial.

The second blizzard lasted three days. Yuke found work to keep Kevin busy, but the days seemed dully alike. The *Clarion* came out as usual on Saturday morning. On Monday school opened again.

12

The Literary

The blizzard left the prairie shrouded in white and the temperature below zero. At school the pupils nearest the stove were too hot. The older ones at the back were too cold and had to keep their coats on. Those youngsters who couldn't go home at noon warmed their cornbread and molasses atop the big stove, and the teacher made tea for everyone. Kevin was glad he could run back to the print shop. Dinner there was usually cornbread and molasses, too, but there was the chance that something exciting had happened.

However, nothing did happen. School, work,

the cold, the leaden skies—everything became monotonous. Kevin almost wished himself back in New
York.

One evening after a week of this, Yuke suddenly
said: "Kevin, me lad, what recitations do you know?"

"By heart?" Kevin asked cautiously. "I don't
know any."

"Then how about learning one? I'm supposed
to scrape up more talent for the next literary."

"What is a literary?"

"Why, it's a meeting to provide intellectual entertainment. We hold one every other Saturday night.
We haven't had one since you've been here on ac-
count of the blizzard. At the last one we had a debate
—among four bachelors. The subject was: 'Resolved;
that a clean, cross woman makes a better wife than
a dirty, good-natured woman.' Do you think that too
frivolous?"

Yuke often asked Kevin's opinion like that.
Kevin suspected he was being teased, but he liked it.

"Not if the women could say what kind of hus-
bands they like," he replied judiciously.

Yuke snorted. "I only wish there were some to
ask! Every girl out here is either married or engaged,

good-natured *or* cross. Getting back to you, how about reciting a poem?"

The bottom seemed to drop out of Kevin's stomach. "I couldn't," he whispered.

"Sure you could! You memorized the case fast enough."

"I couldn't get up in front of everyone."

"It'll be good practice." The finality in Yuke's voice made Kevin know he had no choice. Still, if Yuke thought he could . . .

He licked suddenly dry lips. "How long does it have to be?"

"A couple of pages. Where's your reader?"

Kevin brought it, and Yuke thumbed through.

"How about 'The wreck of the Hesperus'— twenty-two verses?" Yuke suggested.

Kevin looked over Yuke's shoulder. The verses were short. He could use the poem for the next school recitation, too.

So, from being monotonous, the days began to disappear with breathtaking speed. Every evening was spent memorizing. While he fetched water or washed dishes or walked to and from school, some of the lines kept saying themselves over and over in his mind, leading to others he couldn't remember.

Colder and louder blew the wind,
A gale from the Northeast . . .

Here storms came from the North. Straight from the North Pole, with nothing to stop the wind but prairie grass, Yuke said.

Before Kevin crawled into bed Friday night, he said the whole twenty-two verses to Yuke without prompting. If only he didn't forget while he slept!

Saturday morning he trudged through his share of the paper deliveries, repeating the poem twice over while he walked the route. All too soon he and Yuke were taking baths and getting dressed.

"We'll skip supper," Yuke said. "There will be refreshments at the literary, and we'll eat corn pudding when we come home. I'll leave it on the heating stove."

Kevin felt as though someone else was putting his body through its motions. The speaking of the poem was never out of his mind.

Yuke trimmed his beard and blacked his boots. Kevin rubbed the blackened rag over his scuffed shoes.

"What if I forget it?" He had to speak his worry aloud.

"You won't. It's all there in that red head of yours. What about your ancient Irish poets? They could recite for days."

"A long time ago," Kevin muttered.

"Courage!" Yuke slapped him on the back. "Come on, let's go. Two hours from now, it'll be all over."

They put on coats and mufflers and stepped into the frosty night. The town lay luminous in its blanket of snow. Overhead the stars seemed to snap and twinkle in the black sky. The new moon looked so far away and cold it made one shiver. Snow crunched underfoot and the patches of ice were slippery. Yuke was carrying his kerosene lantern, not that they needed it outside; it was to help light the church.

They stomped into the vestibule and hung up their coats. Kevin thought he had never seen such a crowd. Yuke steered him to the front row to sit with the other performers.

He sat in a daze while two people read a dialog. The audience laughed and applauded. A little boy got up and said a poem so short it hardly seemed worth the bother. A young lady sang a song while someone accompanied her on the organ. She was wildly applauded and coaxed to sing another.

It was Kevin's turn. He clomped onto the platform, his shoes making the only sound in the room. He bowed and took his stance, as Yuke had taught him, one hand out of the way in the breast of his jacket, the other free to gesture. He fixed his gaze on the back wall and began. One portion of his mind commanded: speak slowly, keep calm. Nevertheless, he felt sweat sting his armpits.

At last he was saying the final verse.

> *Such was the wreck of the Hesperus,*
> *In the midnight and the snow!*
> *Christ save us all from a death like this,*
> *On the reef of Norman's Woe!*

A final bow and he was able to return to his seat. After the applause, the attention of the audience turned elsewhere. A thin man in much-patched overalls got up and played a jig on a mouth organ. A jig! Now why hadn't Kevin thought of that? He could have danced an Irish jig. Not as well as Uncle Michael, but— his heart missed a beat. He had been so busy, he had all but forgotten Uncle Michael. Tomorrow was Sunday. He would spend the whole afternoon writing a letter.

The music on the mouth organ ended the program. It was time for refreshments: a big jug of cider accompanied by tin cups, which were passed around, and pies, dried apple or dried squash.

Kevin stood beside Yuke, and people he hardly knew told him they enjoyed his recitation. Hannah was there with her brothers. She smiled at him from across the room. He had never felt so lighthearted; the agony was over.

When the dishes were washed and dried, Yuke and the preacher began to choose sides for the spelling contest, which was to be the second half of the program.

The schoolteacher had been asked to give out the words. Yuke's editorial criticizing him had come out in the paper that morning. Kevin trembled to think of the terrible hard words that lay awaiting like traps in the pages of McGuffey's Speller.

The preacher's first choice was Dandy. Yuke chose Mrs. Thayer, so Kevin guessed that she must have a reputation as a fine speller. They went on choosing alternately until all the adults were picked. Kevin hung back. He didn't want Yuke to choose him for fear he'd fail. On the other hand, he didn't want to be chosen for the other side.

The preacher passed over Kevin several times, and at last Yuke called his name. He went to stand at the end of Yuke's row. Across the room Dandy winked at him.

Yuke chose Hannah next. She came to stand beside Kevin. Her face was rounder now and her black eyes sparkled. Her neat black braids were tied by small red ribbons. However, she was looking unhappy.

"I can't spell!" she whispered.

"I can't, either," Kevin said consolingly. "Not the way they do it here." He decided daringly that if he was spelled down soon after Hannah, he would go and sit by her.

Knowing the schoolteacher as they did, the youngsters sensed that he was not in a good mood. No doubt Yuke's editorial rankled.

The poor spellers went down like prairie grass before the wind. The end of the bench next to Hannah was empty when Kevin misspelled his word, but he lost his nerve and went to sit beside Tad Williams. Everyone grew warm with laughter and excitement as one speller after another got his word right or went down. It was impossible not to hold one's breath for the person trying to make his way through tangles of syllables.

At last only the preacher and Dandy remained on one side and Yuke and Mrs. Thayer on the other, but those four went on spelling every word until Mr. Olson closed the speller with a flourish.

"Mrs. Thayer and Gentlemen, you have spelled the last word in the book."

The audience broke into applause. Mr. Olson now brought another list from his pocket. The audience groaned in fearful expectancy. Mr. Olson smiled. Giving out hard spelling words had put him in a better mood.

It was Mrs. Thayer's turn. "Plectospondylous," Mr. Olson pronounced.

"Plectospondylous; p-l-e-c, plec, t-o, toe, plecto, s-p-o-n, plectospon, d-" She hesitated. "i?"

Mr. Olson shook his head.

Mrs. Thayer went down, but everyone applauded because she had lasted so long. Dandy spelled the word correctly. Now it was Yuke's turn.

"Psilanthropy," Mr. Olson said. Yuke spelled it. "Phthisis."

The preacher began: "Phthisis; p-t-h-i-s-" Mr.

Olson shook his head, and it was Yuke's turn again.

"Phthisis; p-h-t-h-y-" Yuke hesitated. Mr. Olson grinned and shook his head. Yuke laughed and limped to his seat amidst clapping. Only Dandy was left!

"Phthisis," he pronounced. "P-h-t-h-i-" He paused dramatically, "ti, s-i-s, sis, phthisis."

Mr. Olson shoved the list into his pocket and led the applause. Dandy had spelled down the town!

He smiled and bowed and shook hands with Mr. Olson and with his team leader, the preacher. In his dark suit with the white ruffled shirt, he looked like an actor. The lamplight gleamed on his blond hair. Altogether, it was the *Clarion*'s night.

Then everyone was getting into wraps and beginning to hurry away.

"This calls for celebration, Dandy," Yuke said. "Come back to the shop with us. We're having corn pudding."

"Come to the saloon with me!" Dandy countered. "That's the place to celebrate. They'll let Kevin in."

Dandy knew Yuke had signed a temperance pledge before he came West, not to drink or chew tobacco, but that didn't stop him from trying to tempt Yuke.

"Nothing doing," Yuke said. He clapped Dandy on the arm. "See you tomorrow morning."

Kevin collected the lantern, and he and Yuke walked home through the crisp, cold night. Mr. and Mrs. Phelps were ahead of them. "What a wonderful evening!" Mrs. Phelps exclaimed. "No wonder we have such a good newspaper."

"Thank you, ma'am." Yuke raised his cap. "Good night."

When they had built up the fire and were eating pudding, Kevin said, "Yuke—you missed that word on purpose, didn't you?"

"What makes you think that?"

Kevin screwed up his face. "I don't know why, I just do. You wanted Dandy to win."

Yuke's burst of surprised laughter told Kevin that he was right, though all Yuke said was: "It was good for Dandy to win. Next time we hold a spelling contest, I hope you'll do better."

Later, snuggled under his comforter and quilt, Kevin lay thinking about his recitation. Speaking it hadn't been so bad.

"Yuke?" he called softly.

"Yeah?"

"Did you like the way I said my piece?"

"Sure I did. I was proud of you."

It was good to fall asleep in the secure knowledge that he had earned tonight's happiness.

13

The Great Easter Storm

Sunday was bitterly cold again. The sweeping wind was merciless, cutting through all layers of Kevin's clothing. He was glad to get back to the print shop after church. After Sunday dinner of baked beans and steamed brownbread, they cleared off the kitchen table and wrote letters—Yuke to Sally, Kevin to Uncle Michael. He sealed the envelope and sat looking at the address: Blackwell's Island Penitentiary, New York City, N.Y. At the drug store —also the post office—Mr. McDonald or his wife would read it. Next thing everyone in town would know about Uncle Michael.

"I wish Mr. McDonald didn't have to see this,"

Kevin told Yuke.

"That's easy fixed. When I meet the train tomorrow, I'll put it in the mail slot in the baggage car. Only the baggage man will see it when he sorts the mail.

Yuke finished his letter and saddled Jack. With Kevin perched behind, they rode out to the claim shanty, mostly because it was someplace to go.

THE WINTER DAYS passed one by one. The Friday night deadline for printing the paper was always there, getting closer and closer. Not that they always made the deadline. Sometimes the paper was late. Subscribers arrived on Saturday morning and the papers were still being printed. Yuke and Dandy would be in ferocious moods—Yuke silent and Dandy grumbling.

But not all was work. The Star Livery Barn owned a sleigh that the Thayer boys themselves often used when there was enough snow. One Saturday after a quiet snowfall, when the weather was bright and promising, they took Hannah the twelve miles to Deer Creek to visit Dolly and Maggie. At church next day Hannah told Kevin and Elizabeth that the little girls had burst into tears on seeing her. They thought she had come to take them back to New York. Because they saw so few people out there, they had grown shy and would hardly talk. "Their homes are one-room claim shanties," Hannah said, "but the folks are nice. Everyone's nice out here. There are so few people that we appreciate each other."

THE SUN CLIMBED higher in the sky. Recess and noontimes grew pleasanter. The eternal prairie wind blew harder, but less cold—a March wind. Bits of green appeared underfoot. Hannah and her brothers took to riding their horses again. Kevin asked to exercise Jack, but Yuke said he must first learn to ride and he didn't have time to teach him.

Flocks of ducks and geese were flying north, except for the few shot down by hungry homesteaders. Two ducks found their way into Yuke's iron stewpot, brought to the *Clarion* as trade for a subscription.

Sometimes the wind was a pleasure—soft, caressing, smelling of freshness and damp earth. Redwing blackbirds appeared in the sloughs. The snow melted, and the ground thawed. The trickles of wagons coming through town became almost a procession, a slow procession because Main Street was an axle-deep ribbon of mud.

Yuke used the *Clarion's* columns to demand a county jail and promote the new baseball team. He joined it, though he seldom took time to attend evening practice. He urged Dandy to join, but Dandy was not to be lured from the saloon's card table.

The loafers at the livery barn began a nonstop game of horseshoes. When Kevin walked home after school, leaping from tuft to tuft of grass to keep out of the mud, the jolly ring of iron shoes against the iron post made it hard to go inside to work. The printshop now seemed dull and demanding. The livery stable was the place to find people and news. Yuke was often there himself. Getting news from back East, Yuke called it, but one afternoon Kevin saw him playing horseshoes.

Kevin had his own news from back East. Uncle Michael had written. He was hoping that there might be a chance to get out of jail early, but he didn't know what he would do once he got out. Kevin wrote back to encourage him to come West.

ON APRIL TENTH Nebraska celebrated Arbor Day. A row of cottonwood saplings was planted around the courthouse square and two were planted in the schoolyard.

Friday, April thirteenth was the first true day of spring, the first day it seemed really warm. Kevin pranced off to school under a blue sky, happy in the thought that the next day was Saturday, and further that in one more week school would close. He could spend his days at the print shop, and evenings he could watch the ball team practice. Also, Hannah had promised to let him ride her pony.

But at noon the sky was overcast and heavy drops were falling. Dandy was alone in the print shop.

"Where's Yuke?"

"Gone to the claim. He's got spring fever."

"What about the paper?" Kevin asked in astonishment. "Tonight's press night!"

Dandy relented and explained. "You know those billheads we printed for the lumberyard? They paid him in lumber. So he borrowed a wagon, hitched up Jack, and is hauling it out there. He's in a hurry to fix that roof. He thinks his girl may come in one day and surprise him."

"So soon?"

"It'll surprise *me* if she does," Dandy said sourly.

They ate the usual noon meal of cornbread and molasses, washed down with milk. Kevin was putting on his jacket to go back to school when something struck the windows with a swish.

Dandy cocked his head. "Sleet! I told Yuke he was rushing the season. Don't go out in that jacket, Red. Put on your coat. Cap, too."

Kevin kept his head down as he ran back to school. Sleet was pelting all the sprouting weeds and grassblades along the path.

No one in the schoolroom could settle down to studying. Icy drops chattered against the panes. Not even Mr. Olson could concentrate on the lessons. The howling wind sounded like a blizzard, though it was too late in the season. When the sound changed and grew quieter, every head raised to listen. The steamy panes made looking out impossible.

Mr. Olson went down the aisle and through the cloakroom to open the door. He was nearly swept from his feet by the blast of wind and snow. Perhaps mindful of Yuke's editorial, he did not hesitate.

"School is dismissed," he said. "Spring or not, this is a blizzard."

By the time the students bounded out of the schoolhouse, all the buildings of the town were blotted out by swirling snow, but not enough had stuck to the ground to obscure the paths. The muddy footprints were just beginning to fill with snowflakes.

Kevin sped to the *Clarion*. He wanted to know that Yuke had returned.

Dandy was there alone. No, Yuke had not come back. They drank tea and waited.

After a while Dandy set his empty cup on the table and stood up. "You and I better start printing the paper."

Kevin discovered you could be stiff with fear and still walk around.

Dandy picked up the heavy page form in which the type was locked and carried it from composing stone to press. This was always a breath-holding moment. No matter how careful the men had been to make sure every letter fitted tightly in its row, and every row fitted tightly in its column, human error was possible. A line might slip or, Heaven forbid, a whole chunk, strewing the floor with tiny leaden letters.

This afternoon Dandy carried the form to the press without accident.

"Yuke won't be back now till the storm's over," he said.

Kevin stood on a box and inked the type. The first sheet was laid on the bed of type. Dandy operated the lever that made paper and type slide under the press and lowered the weight that pressed the paper against the type. A handle raised the weight, and Kevin whisked the printed sheet away so that Dandy could lay on the next one.

Whenever the impression on the paper grew light, Kevin re-inked the type. While he worked, he kept hoping to see Yuke come through the door, though it was foolish to expect him. Please Heaven, he was safe somewhere.

Kevin put potatoes to boil for supper. When half the papers had been run off, he and Dandy sat down to an uneasy meal. Kevin could not stop listening, but all he heard was howling wind. At last he put his fear into words.

"What if he didn't start back in time?"

"Then he's holed up somewhere." Dandy speared a square of salt pork on the point of his knife and put it into his mouth. "By heck, he's not so crazy about printing this paper that he'd risk his neck. It's your newcomers that get themselves lost in blizzards. Oldtimers know how to survive. It doesn't take long to make an oldtimer, either. About one blizzard. Last winter we had a storm like this in November. I was up near Dakota Territory. Another printer and I had a room over the print shop. It was *so* warm that day folks were going barefoot. The next morning we were snowed in. We didn't see another soul for three days. Me and that other feller just set type and played blackjack." Dandy laughed, remembering.

"Didn't you run out of food?"

"Nope. We ran out of copy. We set everything that was on the copy hook, and the boss wasn't there to give us more, so we set our own stuff. Harvey set all the poetry he could remember, and I made up a love story. It was pretty good, too, folks said, when we finally ran it.

"My point is that the editor was prepared for winter. The shop had its supply of coal. The weather bureau at Lincoln recorded seventeen below zero. Some people froze to death." He wiped his plate clean with cornbread and pushed back his chair. "Come on. This paper may not be delivered for days, but it's got to get printed."

Dandy slept in Yuke's bed that night. Throughout the long hours Kevin kept waking to listen to the fury of the wind. Each time he whispered a prayer for Yuke.

Next morning Kevin addressed wrappers and readied the papers for mailing. Dandy broke up the pages and distributed the type into the cases. Without Yuke the day seemed endless. Yuke would have been singing or whistling or cracking jokes.

Darkness came early. After supper Kevin and Dandy sat next to the stove and played checkers. The wind dropped so casually neither of them noticed until they heard a door slam down the street.

Kevin ran to the front window. Scraping away the frost, he saw that the air was clear outside. Snow was drifted deep all across the street. The doctor's house on the far corner was half buried.

Dandy suggested another game of checkers, but Kevin couldn't keep his mind on it. He found himself listening for the back door to open. Yuke could come home now if he was somewhere in town. If he wasn't — Holy Mary, that didn't bear thinking about!

The minutes dragged by. In one jump Dandy took Kevin's last two checkers and won the game. He stood up and yawned.

"I'm going to shovel a path to the outhouse and then turn in."

Kevin banked the fire with a scuttle full of coal and got into bed. Dandy came in, stamping snow off his feet and letting in the cold.

"It's cleared off," he announced. He blew out the lamp. The room filled with the cold light of the full moon.

Kevin felt a surge of hope. Tomorrow the sun would shine and the snow would melt—it was, after all, April—and Yuke would come home. He just had to be all right! Kevin said two Hail Marys before he fell asleep.

Sometime later he was disturbed by more stomping of feet and cold air on his forehead—the only part of him not snuggled under quilts. His first sleepy thought was that it was Dandy, returning from outside. Then he heard Dandy say, "Yuke?"

"Yeah, it's me. Got my bed, have you? Well, you'll have to move over."

"Yuke!" Kevin sat up with a glad cry.

"You're awake, too?" Yuke said. "Then light the lamp for me. Blast it, my fingers are numb."

Kevin jumped out of bed. Shivering, he laid hands on the matches. In a moment yellow flame spread from the match to the wick. Kevin set the chimney over the flame and looked across it. Yuke had brought in a bucketful of snow and was sitting beside the table, pulling off boots and socks. Luckily he'd been wearing his army overcoat. His feet looked bloodless-white. Dandy was getting into his pants, pulling up the suspenders over his underwear.

Yuke began rubbing snow on his feet. The scar from his war wound was blue.

"Frostbit, eh?" Dandy said.

"Looks like it. Feels like it, too. I mean, I can't feel a thing."

"Want some coffee?" Kevin dressed quickly. His heart soared with happiness as he ran into the shop to poke up the fire and set the coffee pot atop the stove. When he returned to the back room, Dandy was offering Yuke the bottle he kept in his coat.

"This'll warm you up faster than coffee," he said.

Yuke waved it away. "You want me to break my pledge?"

"You and your pledge! All right, I'll do it for you." Dandy took a swig, put the cap back on the bottle and stowed it back in his overcoat. "Where have you been, you son-of-a-gun? Kevin was worried to death."

Yuke's lips were cracked and his eyes red-rimmed, but his smile warmed Kevin from head to foot.

"Would you believe it," he said, "I've been holed up in a dugout with a man, his wife, two small children, a cookstove, a table, a bed, trunks, and a team of horses! They made room for Jack, too, bless them!" His lighthearted laugh sounded the first note of cheer in two days. "There wasn't room to *move*, and no heat except what the horses gave off. We stayed in bed the whole two days. Got pretty well acquainted. You can do a lot of talking in two days."

"Did you have anything to eat?" Kevin asked.

"Oh, yes. Bread." Mrs. Williams had baked that morning. They were out of coal before the storm started and were burning hay, but the snow soon covered the haystack. They had enough kerosene to boil water for tea."

"We've got boiled potatoes left from supper," Kevin offered.

"Fry them up!"

"What in Sam Hill were you doing in a dugout?" Dandy asked.

Yuke winced with pain as the blood in his feet began to circulate. "I put the new boards in the roof and shoveled out the sod that had fallen in. When I saw the sleet, I unloaded the rest of the lumber and lit out for town. The snow caught me about halfway.

I remembered that dugout on the edge of Elm Creek so I turned off and got there before the snow hid the wagon ruts. I was sure glad to see that stovepipe sticking up! I guess the Williamses were glad to see me, too. Nevertheless, when the moon came up to-night, I was ready to leave." Yuke shook his head. "Poor lady, she was fresh from the East. She wasn't prepared for pioneering."

He ate the fried potatoes and drank some coffee and then they all went to bed.

In the morning his feet were too swollen to put on his boots, but he said he wasn't going to spend another day in bed. He cut up a motheaten buffalo hide, bound his feet in that and limped around the shop. There wasn't much to do, anyhow, but wait till the town shoveled itself out.

THE NEXT WEEK saw the end of school. Friday was given over to a program, but few parents attended. Everyone in town, it seemed, was getting ready to move to the claims. And Yuke had a letter from Sally saying she was coming in June.

14

Living on the Claim

"Moving day!" Yuke shouted the next Monday morning when he came in from feeding Jack. "Fry up the cornmeal mush. I'll be back by the time it's ready. Got to get a hustle on." He rushed out.

It was spring again. The streets and paths were churning mud.

Yuke returned with Jack hitched to the borrowed wagon. He and Kevin ate a quick breakfast of fried mush and molasses and then loaded ticks, bedding, and dishes into the wagon. Yuke drove around to the front of the general store, and Mr. Phelps helped him carry out an iron bed for Kevin and a little iron stove decorated with curliques.

"My wedding present to Sally," Yuke said.

As they drove out of town, Kevin looked back with some regret. He had never had a chance to try Hannah's pony.

However, the joy of riding beside Yuke across the greening land was soon all-absorbing. The air was fresh and damp and good to breathe. One could see for miles in every direction. Meadowlarks were singing along the way, and redwing blackbirds piped from the draws. Yuke pointed out a hovering sparrowhawk. He promised to take Kevin snipe hunting.

The track was deeply rutted. Wagons were going through town at the rate of fifteen or twenty a day.

The shanty actually looked rather pleasant when they arrived. Grass was springing from the new sod on the roof, and Yuke had installed the glass window. They set up the stove, and Yuke brought a new wooden bucket from the wagon and tied a rope to the bail.

"Come," he said. "Let's take a look at the well." It was boxed in and had a wooden cover. Yuke threw the bucket down and drew it up full of water. "I bought some lime. I figured we'd whitewash the walls before we moved in."

They mixed lime and water in the washbucket. Kevin slapped it on the walls with a brush while Yuke built a shelf for the food. Nails would not hold in the sod wall; he had to hang it from the rafters.

Whitewashed, the room looked pretty good, except for the dirt floor. The sun was high overhead, and they were hungry. Yuke had brought coal, but had forgotten kindling.

"You can fill this basket with dried grass while I pick a mess of greens," he told Kevin.

They twisted grass into hanks, sprinkled kerosene on the coal, and soon the stove was burning off its newness. While greens and potatoes boiled, they moved the table inside.

When at last they sat down to the meal, Kevin decided he liked the shanty. The sun shining through the open door and through the small window lighted the room and perfumed it with the scent of springtime. The wind blew softly across the roof. After the long winter of cornmeal and potatoes, greens were a treat.

They set Kevin's bed next to the one already there, and Kevin spread out the blankets and quilts. Yuke whittled pegs to hang their clothes on and drove them into the sod walls. The beds took up half the room, but there was space to walk between the table and the stove.

"This house is all right if it doesn't rain," Yuke said. "When it rains hard, muddy water drips through the roof." He picked up the spade. "Bring the hoe and come on."

Not far from the house ten acres of sod had been turned with a breaking plow. The battered remnants of last year's cornstalks lay like fallen scarecrows.

"Didn't get much off this patch," Yuke said. "But Uncle Sam says you got to plant ten acres, and that was it. This year, with the sod rotted, it will do better."

Starting at one corner, he began turning over the earth with his spade. Kevin came along behind and crumbled the clods with a hoe. When they had readied a couple of rows, Yuke brought from his pocket some packets of paper tied with thread.

"Sally sent these. She sent flower seeds, too." He showed Kevin how to plant peas and beans and strew tiny lettuce seeds. "While you do that," he said, "I'm going to dig a patch by the door for flowers."

Kevin had never planted anything before. In Ireland, both land and seeds had been too precious to entrust to a child. Now, of course, he was no longer a child, but anyway, there were plenty of seeds, and nobody could say there wasn't plenty of land.

NEXT MORNING Yuke called Kevin out of bed while the sky was still growing light. After breakfast they hitched Jack to the wagon and drove back to town.

"I'm lucky I've got a business," Yuke said. "Can you imagine how hungry we'd get while we waited for that garden to grow?"

At the *Clarion* work went on as usual. Whenever Kevin ran out of other chores he was put to setting type. Each time he set a stickful, he was able to do it with less fumbling.

The rides to and from the claim were the best part of the day. Sitting high on Jack's black rump, Kevin surveyed the prairie and loved it—at least in the springtime. There was beauty in the grass, ever waving before the ever-blowing wind. There was variety in the sky—sometimes a blue, empty bowl, sometimes a bowl filled with fluffy spring clouds or big clouds that billowed up and up till it seemed Heaven must be just beyond. Other times the sky could be a low, ominous presence, dark, menacing, cracking with lightning.

One day a week, usually Tuesday, Yuke left Kevin to work in the house and garden. Kevin did not look forward to those days, but after he got used to the emptiness, he didn't mind them. His main chores were to bake the week's bread, which Yuke put to rise the night before, hoe the garden, and dry the clothes. Also the night before, while Yuke kneaded bread, Kevin built a fire near the well and boiled their dirty clothes in a big iron kettle and rinsed them. Next morning he spread them on the grass to dry. If the light wind grew strong or it began to rain, he rushed them inside.

If he got everything done, he could walk to the creek and swim or fish. Sometimes he did both, leaving the hook baited, the pole propped by a rock, while he took a dip. The creek was wide and shallow and full of crayfish that nibbled at his toes. When he stood on the limestone bottom, the water came to his shoulders. The creek was ugly, with high mud banks cut by floods, but Kevin felt a great fondness for it. Slipping softly down through the wild plum thicket to the bare bank, he was usually able to surprise a kingfisher or a small heron. Yuke called these herons 'shoo-up-the-creeks.' When surprised, they flew up or downstream, never away across the prairie.

ONE SUNDAY AFTERNOON Yuke let Kevin ride Jack. After a few turns around the yard, Kevin grew confident. With Yuke's consent he went for a ride across the prairie.

When he returned, he found three horses tethered to the hitching rail. Tom and Charlie Thayer stood talking to Yuke. Hannah was sitting on the wash bench beside the door. She smiled at Kevin.

Yuke hailed him. "I've invited the Thayers to stay for popcorn and go snipe hunting."

Kevin slid down from Jack. Mindful of what Yuke had taught him about caring for his mount, he led Jack to the sod shelter and rubbed him down with wisps of hay.

When he returned to the house, the bench had been carried inside and everyone was sitting around the stove. Yuke had brought out the cider jug that he kept for visitors. The cider had a nip to it, having been kept since last fall, but for some reason Yuke did not believe that drinking cider broke his temperance pledge. Hannah drank hers from a tin cup, and the boys passed the jug from hand to hand.

Yuke popped three skilletfuls of corn, and they ate the dried apple pie left from Sunday dinner.

Tom finished his piece. "It's almost dark."

Yuke, too, was finished. "Reckon we might as well get everyone in position. Snipe only fly after dark," he explained to Kevin. "I think I've got a couple of gunny sacks in the shed. Kevin and Hannah are new at this, we should give them the easy part."

The Thayer boys nodded.

"What is the easy part?" Kevin asked.

"Holding the sack," Yuke said.

"We have the hard part, driving them in," Tom agreed.

Charlie Thayer giggled.

"Why is he laughing?" Kevin demanded.

"I don't know," Yuke said. "Why are you laughing, Charlie?"

"He's remembering the last time," Tom said. "We drove in so many snipe the fellers who were waiting for them didn't know what to do. They got their bags full and more kept coming. Ain't that right, Charlie?"

"Yah. It was pretty funny."

"Are they good to eat, then?" Kevin asked.

"I'll say they are!" Yuke stood up. "Let's go. With any luck you'll each have a bagful."

Yuke led the way around the hill against which the shanty stood and settled Kevin and Hannah in a small windswept patch near a stand of tall slough grass.

"All you have to do is hold the bags open," Tom repeated. "As soon as it's really dark, we'll start walking towards you. The snipe will run through the grass in front of us. They'll see the open bags and think they're grass tunnels and run in. Once they're in, they ain't got sense enough to turn around. They just keep piling in on top of each other."

"They must be awful stupid birds," Hannah said.

"They are."

"How big are they?" Kevin asked.

"The size of a prairie chicken, but long legged," Yuke said. He and the Thayer boys set off through the grass, away from the shanty.

It was really dark now. Kevin and Hannah knelt on the bare ground, holding the bags in front of them.

Kevin's arms soon grew tired.

"I wonder how long we'll have to wait," he whispered.

Hannah's hushed reply came through the dark. "My arms are weary already."

Kevin changed from kneeling to sitting on one hip. A few hopeful minutes passed.

"Do you hear anything?" Kevin whispered.

"No."

"Maybe we won't hear them till they're right in front of us."

"My brothers couldn't be that quiet if they were paid." Hannah forgot to lower her voice.

They waited a while longer.

"This ground is getting cold," Hannah said.

"Look, there's the moon." A yellow glow was visible at the edge of the prairie. They sat and watched the glow become the moon's rim. The three-quarter moon came up quickly. It threw Kevin's shadow on the ground behind him. He could see Hannah almost as clear as day. No bird was so stupid it would run right into a bag, not even chickens. He jumped to his feet.

"It's a joke! I bet they just want to see how long we'll stay out here."

"Do you think so?" Hannah sounded stunned. "That's why that rat Charlie was laughing!" she cried. "He was laughing at us! Oh! Wait till I tell Papa."

"Let's go back," Kevin said.

He felt Hannah's hand slip into his, and he led her carefully through the grass. It was no fun to walk barefooted into a wild rose or kick an unwary toe against a horse nettle.

Their feet were soaked with dew and Hannah was shivering when they came over the rise and saw the lamplight. Hannah dropped Kevin's hand and ran to the door.

"You were fooling us!"

Yuke lowered the jug from his lips. His eyes were dancing. "The snipe are a little scarce. We stopped off to rest. Where's Kevin?"

"Here." Kevin stepped into the light of the doorway, and Charlie giggled. Yuke and Tom tried to keep their faces straight, but they couldn't. They burst into laughter. Kevin and Hannah had to laugh, too. The joke was on them, but it was a good joke.

Tom got to his feet. "Come on, Charlie, Sis. We'd better head for home. We didn't think it would take you *this* long to catch on." They mounted their horses, shouted good night and rode away.

Yuke came inside still chuckling. "I began to think you were going to stay out there all night." He sat on his bed and pulled off his boots. "That Hannah's going to be a pretty girl. I'll bet she's married before she's sixteen."

"Why?"

"Just a guess. Women are scarce out here."

Lying in bed, Kevin put the future out of his mind and thought about the snipe hunt. He had to laugh again. He and Hannah had been so completely taken in.

"What's so funny now?" Yuke's voice came through the dark.

"The way you fooled us. This has been the best Sunday!"

"Glad you think so. Say your prayers and go to sleep. Tomorrow's Monday."

15

A Change of Plans

One day after dinner, Yuke picked up the stack of handbills that Kevin had been printing that morning and the day before. Piece by piece he had put five hundred sheets on the job press, and kicked the pedal five hundred times.

"Are these ready to deliver?"

"They are," Kevin said.

"Let's go, then!" Yuke smiled. "The trader offered me a horse as the price for printing them. It's yours if you want it."

Kevin's heart leaped. A horse of his own! But he felt he must protest Yuke's generosity. "Don't you need it? I mean, you could sell it."

"No, it's for you. I warn you, it's probably a broken-down nag, but you deserve a horse. You've worked with a will."

"Whoopee!" Kevin's shout was pure joy. He ran out the front door and stood jumping up and down on the boardwalk until Yuke came out.

The horse trader was camped at the edge of town. The horses were staked near his wagon.

Yuke handed the trader the package of handbills. "I should have asked to see the horse," he joked. "You did say it was on its feet, didn't you?"

The horse trader, a thin man with a gray bristly beard, spat a stream of tobacco juice. "If you was to trade hosses with me, I might try to get the better of you, Mr. Smith, but this is a gentlemen's agreement. There she is—that little black mare by the cotton-wood tree. She's got some good years left if you treat her right."

Kevin ran to look at her. The men strolled after him.

She was standing with her head hanging, looking tired. She didn't raise it much when he stroked her. He wished he had a carrot or an apple. Her mane had rather a lot of burrs.

"You're going to be mine," he whispered into her ear.

Yuke came up, spoke soothingly, and pulled down her jaw to see her teeth. She gave him a moment to look before she tossed her head. "Good girl!" He slapped her neck. "She could do with a currying." He turned to the trader. "You don't have an old saddle you'd like to throw in?"

The man scratched his beard. "I might have one I'd be willing to trade for a writeup in the paper."

"Let's see the saddle," Yuke said. "Bring your horse," he told Kevin.

Kevin untied the tether rope from her bridle. With fast-beating heart he led her to the wagon.

The dry old saddle the trader brought out made Yuke shake his head, but they closed the deal. The trader slung a motheaten blanket, and then the saddle onto the mare's back.

"I wouldn't ride her till she's fit to be seen," Yuke advised.

"I can ride her to the claim tonight!" Kevin chortled, as he proudly led her along the road.

"You can curry her and oil your saddle this afternoon, but be quick. I need you in the shop." As usual, a hundred and one things were waiting to be done for tomorrow's *Clarion*.

In the stable Kevin worked happily. Yuke had taught him how to curry Jack, and he gave the mare a thorough going over, clipped the burrs from her mane and tail, brushed dried mud from her hocks, and polished her hooves.

"I'm going to call you Belle," he told her. "That's a stylish name, and so are you."

He swiped two young carrots from the Phelps garden next door and offered them to her. She took them daintily. Kevin gave her hay and a farewell pat, then went into the shop.

Yuke handed him a news item to set. Luckily Kevin could set type now without thinking too hard, because most of his mind was on his wonderful horse.

It was growing dark when he finally got to ride her. Yuke had taken advantage of the long daylight hours to work longer in the shop. At last he was ready to go home.

They rode sedately. It wasn't safe to gallop after dark when neither rider nor horse could see the ground squirrel holes. Kevin felt like a king. The newsboys in New York should see him now! Or even Uncle Michael! A short note had said he really did think he was going to be out of jail soon. So that might be possible. Kevin sometimes wondered what would happen if Uncle Michael did come West. Would he, Kevin, stay on with Yuke or join his uncle? After all Uncle Michael was his only relative. He liked Yuke, though; yet if he was getting married . . . He generally decided in the end not to worry about it. There was no telling what might happen.

He stabled Belle beside Jack in the three-sided sod shelter and pulled carrots for both animals. Reluctantly he told Belle goodnight.

She was still there in the morning, waiting for him. He rode her every chance he got, often bareback. They grew accustomed to each other, and he took her for long expeditions over the prairie. Sometimes he rode with Hannah and her brothers. Nothing in his life, he sometimes decided, had ever been so good.

MAY SLIPPED into June. In spite of rabbits and ground squirrels, the garden was growing well. The prairie was beautiful—a blowing green carpet, with wild roses fluttering in the windswept grass.

"Look at this country!" Yuke exclaimed one morning. "Sally's going to miss the best part of the year if she doesn't come soon."

"Doesn't it stay like this?" Kevin asked.

"No," Yuke admitted. "It gets hot and dry. Some professors say it will be better when the sod gets plowed. They say that will bring the rainfall."

June was half over before Sally's letter arrived. Kevin brought it from the post office with the other mail. Yuke tore open the envelope and glanced at the single sheet. He looked up with a grin.

"She's coming the first of July!"

Dandy was working at his case. "I'll be pushing on about that time," he announced.

"Because I'm getting married!" Yuke exclaimed.

Dandy nodded. "Can't abide marriages."

"But she'll help in the shop, too!"

"Can't abide a woman in the shop, either."

Yuke was silent, his pleasure dampened by Dandy's reaction.

"If that's the way you feel," he said finally.

"Kevin is getting pretty handy, you know."

Kevin felt himself swell with pride. Praise from Dandy was something he had never expected to hear.

"You'll stay for the wedding, at least?" Yuke asked.

Dandy shook his head. "I didn't figure to."

"He's afraid that girl at the saloon will get ideas,"

Yuke told Kevin.

Dandy sighed. "Yeah, she wants to get hitched. That's one reason for going."

Yuke consulted the calendar. "Jumping Jehoshophat, the first is on a Friday. Oh, Dandy, be a sport! See me through that week. Every business in town will be advertising for the Fourth. You don't have to come to the preacher with us, but I can't get out a paper the day she arrives! I'll be meeting the train and showing her the claim—"

Dandy shrugged. "Why not? Not having any plans, it's no trouble to change them."

Kevin tried not to think about her coming, but it was difficult. Yuke didn't announce it in the paper, but the gossip got around. All the women were thrilled that a new woman was coming to town, and the men were always kidding Yuke about not having to do his own cooking in the future. The first of July grew nearer and nearer and still Kevin could not feel glad, as he knew he should. Maybe Uncle Michael would come and take him away. That would be one solution. But he wasn't sure it was a solution he wanted.

"TODAY'S THE DAY!" Yuke cried, rolling out of bed

the morning Sally was due. Riding to town, Kevin did his best to appear happy. But inside he was so upset he could hardly talk.

Yuke spent the morning rushing in and out. He brought his newly pressed black suit and hung it in the back room and went off to get a haircut and his beard trimmed. Next time Kevin saw him he was heading for the hotel to order the wedding dinner for Saturday noon. His limp seemed worse than usual.

He was back for their noon meal and then he puttered around the shop. At last it was time to go to the station, if the train was on time. Kevin went with him, leaving Dandy to put the paper to bed and lock up the forms, ready for printing.

The train was supposed to arrive at two o'clock, but as usual it was an hour late. The regular crowd gathered. The train's arrival almost always provided the day's greatest excitement and for some a possibility of added income. There was a chance that some rich Easterner might hire a man to drive him out to look for land. And two people in town made a business of selling food to the travellers—fresh rolls, baked potatoes, hard-boiled eggs.

Smoke from the engine could be seen long before the train appeared, a dark speck where the rails met the horizon. It drew near and at last ground to a halt in front of the station, hissing, letting off steam.

People began to file out of the two passenger cars. They crowded round the sellers of food.

The conductor turned to Yuke, who was waiting beside him. "Here's your Chicago paper. The telegraph says grasshoppers are bad further out. Had any here?"

"No more than usual." Yuke was looking eagerly at the descending passengers.

The conductor shook his head. "A plague of grasshoppers wouldn't surprise me. Well, besides travellers and emigrants today, we've got another load of paddies going out to lay track."

The words were scarcely out when Kevin's quick ears heard the voices of Irishmen. They were surging from the last car. Even as he turned to look, he heard a shout.

"Kevin, me boy!"

A man burst from the crowd. It was Uncle Michael! He was wearing a dark jacket, denim trousers stuffed into worn boots, and a cap. His face was whiskery below and pale above, his blue eyes laughing. He pounded Kevin on the shoulder.

"I'd have known that red hair anywhere. The

saints preserve us! Had I known what an empty country this is, even a dollar a day wouldn't have coaxed me to take this job, but you were out here. Kevin, how are you? Faith, I know how you are, since you've written regular. Say something, boy!"

Kevin could only grin. Yuke was still watching the people emerging from the parlor car. Kevin tugged at his sleeve. "Yuke— My uncle's here!"

Yuke shook hands, his eyes still on the emerging passengers.

"He's expecting his sweetheart," Kevin whispered to Uncle Michael. "He's getting married tomorrow."

Yuke looked at Uncle Michael long enough to say, "Are you stopping off, Mr. O'Halloran?"

Uncle Michael scratched his head. "Faith, I wasn't expecting to meet Kevin right here at the station. But since I have, maybe I'll go on with the train. 'Tis grateful I am for your care of him."

"He's earning his keep," Yuke said shortly.

The passengers were all off now, even those merely out to stretch their legs. Yuke turned back to the conductor.

Kevin smiled shyly at Uncle Michael. "I'm glad they let you out."

"No gladder than I! Good behavior, they called it. They told us about these railroad jobs, with free passage west, and when I learned the line went to Nebraska, I hopped aboard. Are you ready to go on, me boy?"

"Go on?"

"Sure, ain't we going together? I've got you a job as cook's helper, two bits a day. This carload is a whole new crew, going out to replace men who left for the silver mines. I figured you and me would see the Indians and the buffalo and work long enough to get a stake, as they call it, and then we could go to Nevada, too. They do say the silver's there, waiting to be picked up."

Kevin's heart leaped. What an adventure that would be! "I've already got a horse," he said. Maybe this was the answer to Sally's coming. But he couldn't just leave, not when Yuke had been so good to him. "Could I ride out and meet you in a couple of days?"

"That's fine! They tell me we'll reach the end of the line tonight. So no doubt you could ride out there in a day or so."

"I could follow the railroad tracks!"

People began getting back on the train. Yuke was standing alone, his hands in his pockets, looking as though the sun was hurting his eyes.

"I'd best be taking me seat, too," Uncle Michael said. "They start off without warning. I reckon the trainmen like to see us run." He clasped Kevin in a fierce hug. "Perhaps 'tis wrong in me to coax you away. Maybe you ought to continue your schooling."

Kevin shook his head. "I'd rather come with you. He's getting married."

"But seemingly not tomorrow," Uncle Michael said with a twinkle. "Sure, and I'll look for you then in a day or two." He stepped aboard, waved and disappeared inside the car.

16

A Plague of Locusts

The train pulled out, leaving a feeling of emptiness. The people who had come to meet it drifted away. Yuke and Kevin started back along the dusty road.

Kevin's thoughts chased themselves round and round. What a surprise it had been to see Uncle Michael! He wished they'd had more time at the station, but it was fine to know he'd be seeing him soon. And out of prison, too! It was fine to know he really was out of prison. Only did he really want to leave Cottonwood? Kevin's stomach lurched at the thought. Was that because he didn't want to leave? He knew it would be fun to go West with Uncle

Michael and he had said he would, but his father would have said he'd do better to stay in Cottonwood and go to school. But his father wasn't the one who had brought him to America. Uncle Michael was the only family he had now. Except Yuke; he felt like family. That was another thing. What would Yuke say?

He hardly noticed the silence until Yuke spoke.

"If something went wrong, or she missed the train in Chicago, she'd have telegraphed. Wouldn't you think she would have telegraphed?"

"Maybe she didn't know how." Kevin realized he wasn't the only one with trouble. Poor Yuke! He must be terribly disappointed. He would have to tell everyone that he wasn't being married tomorrow.

"Her folks talked her out of it at the last minute. That's what happened," Yuke said bitterly.

"Maybe she didn't get packed in time," Kevin offered.

"Then why didn't she let me know?"

"Maybe she wrote you a letter."

"Maybe. I'll go to the post office. McDonald should have the mail sorted by now."

They walked on in silence. Kevin noticed a little gray cloud in the west, like smoke from a prairie fire. He felt sorry for whoever was in its path because the wind was blowing hard today. They reached Main Street and separated.

"Tell Dandy I'll be there in a few minutes," Yuke said.

At the shop Dandy had the press ready to run. Kevin fell to work helping him.

"Well—?" Dandy urged. "What's she like?"

"She didn't come."

"Didn't come! Where's Yuke?"

"At the post office."

"Humpf!" Dandy snorted. "He's a brand snatched from the burning, if only he knew it."

"If she doesn't come at all, will you stay?"

"I might." Dandy spaced his words between crashes of the press. "Cottonwood's not a bad place."

That made Kevin feel better. At least he wouldn't be leaving Yuke all alone.

"What have you got such a long face for?" Dandy asked.

"I'm sorry for Yuke," Kevin said, but he realized that was only part of the reason. The other part was that he didn't want to leave the print shop and Yuke. Especially now.

When Yuke came through the front door, an

opened letter in his hand, Kevin knew by the way his shoulders slumped that the letter held bad news. Dandy stopped working the press.

"She's changed her mind." Yuke flung his hat and letter atop his cluttered desk. "She doesn't want to live in a sod house. Great Heaven, everybody out here had to live in a soddy or a dugout or a one-room shack to begin with. It wouldn't be forever." He limped aimlessly about the shop, drank from the dipper and tossed it back into the waterbucket. "You fellows print the paper. I'm going for a ride."

Suddenly the room grew dark. Outside the sunlight had faded.

"Hey," Dandy said, "you'll get wet if you do."

Yuke paused in his pacing. The wind pelted raindrops against the windowglass, but when Kevin looked, the sill wasn't wet. It was sprinkled with grasshoppers. There was a curious fluttering hum in the air.

"That's funny!" he exclaimed.

Out in the street a woman screamed. Then shouts and the sound of galloping came through the side window.

"Another runaway?" Dandy was again feeding the press.

Kevin went to the window to look. He stared in disbelief. "Grasshoppers!" He watched with astonishment as insects came like driven snow, covering the weeds, the street, the roof of the saloon across the vacant lot. "It's raining grasshoppers!"

Dandy and Yuke came to stand beside him. The insects struck the windowpanes with the sound of hail.

"Shut the window!" Dandy came out of his stupor. "That's what all the screaming was about. Here—I'll close the windows. You shut the shed, Kevin, before they scare the horses."

"They've been getting this down in Kansas, according to the papers." Yuke moved to the front door and stood looking out, as little concerned as though he were watching a play.

Kevin ran out the back. He had to cross a crawling carpet of grasshoppers to get to the shed. At every step they were under his bare feet. His toes recoiled. The grasshoppers' armored heads and wings were so hard he could kill one only by grinding it under his heel. While he crunched one, a dozen more were landing on his hair and shoulders and crawling up his legs, digging in their sharp barbs. Phelps's chickens were having a heyday.

Grasshoppers were pouring into the shed, hopping into the manger and on the horses. Kevin closed the shutter that covered the window. With both door and window closed, the only light came through the cracks. Kevin grabbed a broom and tried to sweep the grasshoppers into a pile and out the door, but a great many escaped. He gave up and hurried back into the shop. He didn't want to miss any of the excitement.

"A plague of locusts," Yuke was shouting. "Right out of the Bible. This country is cursed!"

"Oh, come now," Dandy tried to soothe him. "Don't condemn the whole country because your sweetheart went back on you. Maybe you're luckier than you know."

Yuke clapped his hat on his head and threw Dandy a furious look. "I suppose *you* know! You don't know a darned thing!" He limped out the back door and slammed it.

"He shouldn't take Jack out in this," Kevin worried.

"Let him go," Dandy said. "Maybe the grasshoppers will take his mind off his woman trouble."

All the time that Kevin was doing his part of printing the paper, his mind kept turning round and round the idea of going West. How exciting it must be—all that bustle of men and teams, and every day the rails stretching closer to the mountains. The Union Pacific line already went to California, but the Burlington was building northwest to other wild places. He wondered where everyone went when winter came.

From time to time Dandy stopped working the press so they could take a look at the grasshoppers. It was unbelievable! They were eating all the weeds in the lot next door. In places they were inches deep.

"They sound like cows in a cornfield," Dandy remarked.

A wagon passed up the street, the driver shouting and cursing his horses, which shied and baulked as flying 'hoppers struck their heads.

A few men drifted in to discuss this latest affliction, but Dandy didn't stop work and they drifted out again.

Kevin turned over in his mind the words he would use to tell Yuke he was leaving. He wondered if Yuke would feel bad. It didn't seem very nice to walk out on him now.

For once the press run went smoothly. Folding *Clarions* for addressing, Kevin realized he was doing it for the last time. He felt sad.

By sunset they were finished. Dandy said good-night and went off to supper at the hotel. Kevin saddled Belle. The long summer evening had barely begun, but the grasshoppers had settled for the night, so thick most places they were like a horrible, crawling carpet. As Kevin rode out of town, he saw fires here and there. People were throwing insects on the flames by the basketfull, but of course the grasshoppers didn't burn very well and gave off a vile smoke.

He crossed the railroad tracks. The road from there on was mostly through prairie grass, which the grasshoppers didn't seem to go for. He saw three riders coming towards him and recognized Hannah's pony with its white stockings. Tom and Charlie were with her.

"Howdy, Kevin." Their greetings were subdued. All three were sagging in their saddles. They were close enough now for Kevin to see scratches all over their hands and feet, even their faces. Their clothes were dirty and stained.

"What have you been *doing?*" he cried.

"Fighting grasshoppers on our claim," Tom answered.

"But how did you get so scratched?"

"From the barbs on their legs. What have *you*

been doing to stay so clean?"

"Clean!" Kevin's hands and shirts were never free of printer's ink. "I was printing the paper."

"Lucky you!" Charlie said. "You should have seen those 'hoppers. They ate *everything*, even down into the ground—the turnips—"

"And all the onions—" Tom put in. "We tried covering up the garden and Ma's flowers with bedclothes, but they started eating the bedclothes. We tried killing them with shovels, but the more we killed, the more they came."

"And they ate the dead ones," Hannah added. "Ugh!"

"They ate the shirt off the scarecrow, and then they started on the wooden crosspiece," Tom said.

"Aw—" Kevin protested.

"They did!" Charlie backed up his brother. "Ask Hannah! They even chewed up the hoe handle and the scythe."

Hannah nodded. "They got in the shanty, too. Ugh! I'm glad we have a house in town! Did Yuke's sweetheart come? I bet she wishes she hadn't."

"She didn't come. Yuke got a letter. She isn't coming."

"Oh, poor man!"

The boys were silent, embarrassed.

"You know who did come, Hannah? My Uncle Michael. He's going out to work on the tracks. He wants me to meet him out there."

The Thayer boys were clucking to their horses. "Hannah, we better get on home," Tom said as their mounts began to move. "It's past suppertime."

"And I'm starving," Charlie announced.

"I'll catch up," Hannah called after them. She turned back to Kevin. "Are you going?"

"He's my uncle."

"But what about Yuke?" Hannah looked disapproving.

"Well, when I saw Uncle Michael at the train, I still thought Yuke was getting married."

"But now he's not! And you were learning to be a printer. You're just going to leave that to work with a bunch of rough men are you? What about school?"

Kevin had no answer. In a way, Hannah was right. Yuke needed him now, but so did Uncle Michael. He couldn't be both places. He sighed.

"Couldn't you just go for the summer?" Hannah asked.

"And come back when school starts? Yeah, maybe." Kevin stared at her, his heart lightened. It seemed the perfect answer. He wasn't sure what railroad camps did in the winter, anyway. As for going to look for silver—well, if so many men had already gone, it didn't seem very likely that the latecomers would find any.

"I've got to go." Hannah clucked to her pony. Over her shoulder she called, "If you write to me, I promise to write back!" The pony broke into a trot. Kevin watched her ride away, her bare brown feet clasping the pony's sides, her braids bouncing.

I *will* write to her, he promised himself. Anyhow, maybe he'd be coming back in the fall. It depended on what Yuke said about the whole idea. He didn't mind so much telling him now. If he went, it wouldn't be forever. And Yuke would understand why he had to go.

When he rode into the yard, he thought at first that Yuke wasn't there. Even in the fading light the devastation was awful. The brush looked as bare as if it were winter. No leaf or small branch was left anywhere. In the garden, only holes remained where the carrots and turnips had been growing so prettily.

Jack was in the shed, however. Both the door and the window of the soddy were shut. Yuke must be holed up inside.

Kevin shook sleeping grasshoppers out of every handful of hay before he gave it to Belle. Jack had his hay already.

"Yuke?" Kevin said when he pushed open the door of the house.

There was no answer, but when his eyes accustomed themselves to the deeper darkness, he made out a figure stretched on the bed.

Making as little noise as possible, he lighted the lamp. By the lamplight he saw that Yuke was not asleep. He was lying with his hands behind his head, staring at nothing. Clearly he was in a bad mood. Kevin wished Yuke had at least done something about supper. What was there to eat, anyhow? He found potatoes in the bin, built a fire, and mixed biscuits. There was molasses for the biscuits and salt for the potatoes and that would be it. The room grew so hot he had to open the door and window to the mosquitoes. While the potatoes were boiling and the biscuits were baking, he went and sat on the other bed, determined to say what had to be said.

"Yuke . . ."

Yuke grunted.

"You remember my uncle was on that train? Well, he wants me to follow him out to where they're laying track. I sort of said I would. I didn't know then that your sweetheart wasn't coming—not at all. I thought maybe I could go for the summer—"

"What?" At last Yuke turned his head; his eyes focused on Kevin.

Kevin couldn't guess whether Yuke had listened to anything he said. He took a deep breath and said it all again.

"West?" Yuke echoed when he ended .

"Just till cold weather," Kevin repeated. "I don't see how they can work during the winter."

"West!" Yuke exclaimed. His eyes brightened. He sat up and swung his feet to the floor. "West, by George! Why don't we both go?"

"But—but—" Kevin was too surprised to do anything but stammer.

"Why not?"

"What about the paper?"

"It won't hurt to skip a week. It's come out regular ever since I took over. Let folks miss it once."

"Oh! I thought you meant go West for good."

"No, I guess not." Yuke sounded wistful, but he went on to say, "You didn't want to go for good, either, did you?"

"No—" Kevin understood that they both felt

the same way: it would be fun to toss up everything and travel on, but foolish. He would be throwing away his chance for schooling, and for printer's training. Yuke would be giving up what could be a good business. But right now they both had a need to leave for a while.

Yuke stared through the open door into the dark, his eyes dreamy. "I could ride out that way and look around." He brought his gaze back to Kevin. "And we could see what the railroad camp is like. If it's all gambling and drinking, like I've heard, it's no place for you. Your uncle will probably agree with me. On the other hand, maybe the wildness is exaggerated. We can pay your uncle a visit and see."

"And if it's all right?"

"Then you can work till they close. School doesn't get started till after fall plowing. The railroad camp must close down about the same time."

"If I stay and work, what will you do?"

"Maybe I'll circle down into Kansas and see how bad the grasshoppers are there. The subscribers would like to read about that. I might even go on to Denver and see the mountains. Maybe take *two* weeks."

"What if the camp's too rough?" Kevin began to hope it might be. Yuke's trip sounded more exciting than working.

"You can make the trip with me, if you want to."

For the first time all day Kevin began to feel happy. What fun it would be to ride west with Yuke! Not only that, it would give them something to talk about all next winter. And maybe Uncle Michael would come back when the work ended. Surely he couldn't hunt for silver when the ground was covered with snow.

Yuke was apparently thinking the same thing, for he said, "Your uncle might want to come back here for the winter, though there'll be nothing for him, unless he saves his money. Hey, is that biscuits I smell? Let's eat!"

NEXT MORNING Yuke was still of the same mind.

"We can just as well leave today," he said when he returned from watering the horses. Kevin was cooking mush. "Dandy did say he'd stay on for a while didn't he? Maybe he can take care of things at the shop. As for here, even the water's not fit to drink, but there's a good wind blowing. It ought to move the 'hoppers on."

Sure enough, the creatures were taking to the air. They made a haze over the rising sun. The wind was blowing strongly from the northwest. They had eaten just about everything in sight. The hollyhocks and cornflowers might never have been. The two little apple trees had lost not only their leaves but their bark; they would probably die. Only the native prairie grass remained and the row of castor beans. Kevin put his summer clothes together in a blanket—shoes, underwear, spare shirt. His winter coat from the society could stay in Yuke's trunk, safe from moths.

Yuke was packing, too.

"Should we take some food?" Kevin asked.

"We'll get meals along the road. Homesteaders are always glad to earn two bits."

They tied their bundles to their saddles with twine and were ready to leave. Yuke closed the soddy's door.

"I'll pick up my type stick and composing rule at the shop, just in case, and tell Dandy what we have in mind," Yuke said. "He may want to come along, but I hope not. I hope he'll stay and look after business. Though after yesterday's visitation, I don't suppose there'll be much business. If the crops are ruined, people will begin flocking back east. I'll have to see the preacher, too, and tell him I'm not getting married. By George, boy, I'm glad you talked me into leaving town!"

Kevin laughed.

Yuke grinned. "Well, you gave me the idea. I won't have to put up with any condolences *or* ribbing. By the time I get back, they'll have something else to talk about."

With a pencil he lettered a sign on a whitewashed board and nailed it to the door: GONE FOR TWO WEEKS. "There—that should hold the place against anyone fool enough to want to move in."

They set off across the dew-wet prairie toward town. It seemed the best morning in the world to be going somewhere.